ISOBEL

JULIE KENT

To Rusty and Lexi:
You both taught me how to love
more than I knew was possible.

Being your mom is the greatest gift of all!

For Auntie Margie-
Your strength is beautiful!
I love you always and forever!

The oldest and strongest emotion
of mankind is fear, and the oldest
and strongest kind of fear is
fear of the unknown...

-- *H.P. Lovecraft*

PART I

The bazaar marked the beginning of the autumn season in Clairemont as vendors and store merchants got together on the sidewalks of downtown Main Street for the yearly tradition to showcase their crafts and merchandise. The bazaar was usually very busy as the organizers of the event were extremely careful to schedule it during a time when there was nothing else going on in the town of Clairemont, or the surrounding areas.

The people who lived there were so supportive of the event because it brought people together, which was something they needed from time to time because the town was centrally located in the middle of absolutely nothing. You had to drive at least forty-five minutes to an hour if you wanted to find any signs of civilization.

Isobel was in her bedroom changing out of her nightgown into some jeans and a sweater to wear to the Clairemont Bazaar. She wrapped an elegant pink scarf over her long blonde hair and headed out of her bedroom door. It was a little chilly that October morning so she also grabbed a light jacket and draped it over her arm so she would have it just in case she wasn't warm enough. Ready to go (by herself as usual), she headed downstairs to the front door where she knew her purse was sitting on a small table right next to the front door. Isobel was a creature of habit, always making sure she put her belongings in the same place every day (she never knew when the time might come that she would have to leave abruptly).

Isobel was digging in the bottom of her purse searching for her keys when she was suddenly grabbed from behind by her hair. She quickly turned around to confront her attacker as she thought to herself:

Damn; I was as good as out the door. Those damned keys!

"Where the hell do you think you're going?" It was her husband, Tom. He never wanted her to go anywhere. "Put the purse down," he said, "you're not going anywhere!"

Isobel slowly started to put her purse down on the table, but she looked up at him instead (which was something she knew she would regret), "It's the bazaar, Tom," she took a step back from him, "I go every year," she said and then looked down at the floor and braced herself because she knew what was coming.

Tom still had ahold of her arm and started squeezing it so hard she knew there would surely be another bruise to cover up. "I SAID PUT IT DOWN!" he screamed as he pulled on the arm he was holding and slammed her into the adjacent wall so hard a picture toppled off its nail and went crashing to the floor.

Isobel stood there with her back up against the wall just looking down at the glass that had shattered and surrounded the two of them. It was a photo of her and Tom on their honeymoon in Bermuda. They were having a romantic dinner by the water and they had their server take the photo. Isobel thought of that day often as she looked at that picture from time to time and wondered when and why things had changed so drastically between the two of them. She loved him, but she had become terrified of him.

Tom kicked some of the pieces of glass into the wall and yelled, "Clean this shit up," before throwing her down on the floor where some glass sliced her knees when she landed on it. He walked away, leaving her on the floor in tears. He reappeared in less than a minute with a broom and dust pan, which he threw down on the floor next to her. The broom handle hit her in the head causing her head to jolt backwards and hit the wall again.

When he walked away again, Isobel picked up the broom and tried to get to her feet on shaky legs. She was able to get the mess swept up off the floor and then she went into the half bathroom that was right in the small hallway that led to the front door. She dumped the broken shards of glass into the wastebasket and cleaned up her bloody knees with a washcloth that was hanging on the towel rack.

When she was finished, she peaked out of the bathroom door to try to see where Tom was, but he was nowhere in sight. She was so nervous, but she had to get out of the house. She was not going to miss the bazaar due to this man again (he beat her so badly the previous year, she couldn't go anywhere for a while). With her heart pounding like thunder in her chest and her legs feeling like jelly, Isobel made her way out the front door without being noticed. She decided to walk because she did not want Tom to hear the car starting up in the driveway. His sense of hearing was like that of a bat.

Main Street was only six blocks from where the Parrish's lived, but the walk seemed longer that morning because her knees started to ache almost immediately when she started her journey to the bazaar on foot. It could have been because she walked quickly as to not be seen by Tom, who she prayed would not look out the window until she was safely out of sight, but it was most-likely the fresh cuts and bruises on her knees that were the cause of her knee pain.

There was a steady stream of cars that passed her as she made her way to the bazaar and she just knew they were probably going the same place she was. She always went alone. Well, she did *everything* alone because Tom would not allow her to have friends. She also did not want to have to explain her bruises and tears to anyone, so seclusion was easiest for her.

As she neared the event, the aroma of popcorn and cotton candy filled the air. There were food vendors set up every year that gave the bazaar the atmosphere of a circus or fair. There was also a clown handing out bright red balloons to all of the children. He was standing on the corner as soon as you entered Main Street. He was dressed as the traditional party clown-type with the big red shoes, big red hair, and a big red round nose in the center of his colorfully painted face. There was also a station set up right next to him where a woman was painting kids' faces. It was a cute set up that led people into the bazaar.

Isobel smiled as she walked past them and made her way to the vending tables. There were crafters selling things from homemade clothing to Halloween decorations. There was one older lady who was there every year who knitted the most amazing afghans. Everyone loved them and there was probably one of her afghans in just about every household in Clairemont. Isobel bought one a couple of years ago but Tom set it on fire to teach her a lesson one day. He came home from work and dinner was not finished. He found her asleep on the couch wrapped up in that afghan and said she needed to pay more attention to her household duties, and less attention to lounging around on the sofa. After punching her in the stomach, he took the blanket outside and threw it into their fire pit, which he ignited with lighter fluid and a match. He made her watch as the afghan instantly went up in flames.

As Isobel continued to walk along the sidewalk passing the face painting station, she stopped at the next vending table which was selling danishes and coffee. She had left the house in such a rush that morning to avoid further confrontation with her husband that she didn't have a chance to have any coffee, which was something she had a bit of an unhealthy addiction to. It was not unusual at all for her to have three cups of the caffeinated beverage in the morning, and sometimes she would have more in the evening. She was like a heroin addict when she walked into a Starbucks. With her cup of Joe in hand she walked on to the vendors.

She walked past the afghan lady without even slowing down her pace. She could barely look at the woman since the fire pit episode. She felt so bad because a lot of hard work had gone into the blanket that had turned to ash in Isobel's back yard in a matter of seconds.

She kept walking, not really paying attention to any of the vendors because the morning run-in with Tom was weighing heavily on her mind. She didn't want to get caught up in any conversation with anyone. She had cuts and bruises she was also trying to keep covered up and did not want to explain them to anyone, not that anyone in Clairemont would ask her anyway. She had no real friends; Tom made sure of that by not giving her any freedom to do what she wanted.

Isobel stopped briefly on the sidewalk to tip her head to sip her coffee, when something caught her eye. There was a table set up at the end of a line of clothing vendors that she had never seen before. They were not selling clothing. It appeared as though they had computer stuff. It got her attention because a computer was something Tom would not let his wife have because it would allow her access to the outside world. She could never go to a store to inquire about one because he would find out. He knew all of the business owners in town. The people he did not know were the ones who came to the yearly bazaar because he never went with her, and most of the vendors were from out of town.

As she got closer to the table she could read the sign that was propped up in a chair in front of the business, which displayed their business name: *Annie's Odds 'n Ends.* There was a young girl sitting behind the table next to an older gentleman. The girl was in a wheelchair and Isobel assumed the man was her father; they kind of looked alike. They had a set-up that was U-shaped with three tables and an opening for them to go in and out of the display. Isobel was amazed at all of the different items she saw. They had things from complete computer set-ups, to keyboards, to any little gadget you could think of that one might need to add to their electronic obsession.

Isobel went right up to the table, and was instantly drawn to an open-boxed display on one of the side tables. It looked like one of those old typewriters that was used back in the 1940s or 50s. She wasn't sure what time period it was from, but it was old. She walked over to the girl in the wheelchair, who looked up at her and smiled.

"Welcome to our stand, Miss," the girl said.

"Thank you." Isobel said, "Where are you guys from? I don't remember seeing you here before."

"We have a shop in Philadelphia," the girl said. "We were passing through and decided to come to this bazaar."

"Well, I'm glad you did, What is your name?"

"I'm Clara, and that is my father," she said as she

pointed to the older gentleman who was now talking to someone about a keyboard.

"I wanted to ask about the box over there," Isobel pointed to the open box with the typewriter in it.

Clara put her finger up in a motion that told Isobel she would just be a minute. She wheeled herself over to where her father was. She interrupted him and was back in less than two minutes. "My dad will help with that. It is too heavy for me to move."

Isobel watched as the man finished his conversation at the other end of the table and slowly approached her. She didn't know why, but he appeared to have a look of concern on his face. He got to where she was and put his hand on his daughter's shoulder. He kind of half- smiled at Isobel and looked at the box she was inquiring about. Then he looked back at her and asked, "Can I help you?"

Isobel hesitated because he gave her a slight feeling of uneasiness, but then she responded, "I was interested in looking at the typewriter in that box over there."

He looked at her as if she was asking about something illegal. "That one," he hesitated, "is special."

"How so?" Isobel asked.

"It is the oldest piece I have in my collection," he said. "We have had that one for a long time and it has been through a lot with us."

The man was talking about the typewriter as if it were human, which only made Isobel more curious about it.

"Can I look at it, Sir? Is it for sale?"

"It is...," he creepily said, "but I can't let it go for less than four hundred dollars."

While they talked, Clara looked at Isobel with desperate eyes that were on the verge of tears. Isobel noticed her and looked back toward the man, "That's a lot of money," she said, "I'll have to think it over."

She walked away from *Annie's Odds 'n Ends* and strolled along, looking at some decorative crafts for the autumn season. She was no more than four or five tables away when she felt a slight tug on the back of her jacket. She looked back and was surprised to see the young girl, Clara, had wheeled to where she was walking. Clara was crying and Isobel kneeled down to comfort her. She gave her a tissue she had in her pocket and put her arm around the girl's shoulders.

"What's wrong, honey?" Isobel asked in a soothing, motherly kind of way.

"Don't buy that machine," Clara said. "It's bad."

Isobel saw the despair in her eyes. "Why," she asked, "What do you mean?"

Clara looked down at her legs, "This chair..," she said. "The typewriter is the reason I have to be in it." Her tears grew heavier. "It did this to me," she yelled.

"That's impossible." Isobel said, "How?"

"Just don't buy it," Clara said. "And if you do, please don't use it."

"Let's get you back to your dad, sweetie," Isobel said as she grabbed the handlebars on the back of Clara's wheelchair.

Not another word was spoken on their journey back to the vending table where Clara's father was waiting for her. Apparently, she told him she was just going to get a drink. He was surprised to see her return without a drink, and with Isobel pushing her along.

"I see you came back," he said.

Isobel looked at Clara and then back up at him. "I'll take it!"

It was decided that Arthur (the man who owned *Annie's Odds 'n Ends*) would deliver the typewriter to Isobel the following day while her husband was at work, because there was no way she would be able to carry it home. Not to mention; she did not want Tom to see her new purchase before she could come up with a good explanation for why she bought it, and what it was for. She always had to justify her actions to him, and most of the time, it didn't matter. She got her ass beaten to a pulp anyway.

That day when she got home from the bazaar, she lucked out. Tom was sleeping off a six- pack on the couch (the remnants of which were obvious by the empty bottles on the coffee table), snoring heavily as she tiptoed upstairs to her bedroom. She took off the clothes she had worn to go out and replaced them with some ragged old sweats, which Tom preferred her to wear as to not attract any of their male neighbors. Isobel was very attractive, with a slender figure and long blonde hair, which made Tom very jealous when anyone looked in her direction. It was easier for her to dress like a slob around the house, than to dress nice and get the shit beaten out of her because John from next door happened to glance in her direction. One time when they were at the hardware store picking up a few things, the clerk who waited on them simply asked her how she was doing. That tiny encounter resulted in a broken nose for her by dinner time, when Tom slapped her so hard in the back of the head that she fell on the floor face-first. Her nose had a permanent bump in the middle of it from that little love tap.

Tom slept until almost nine which gave Isobel time to enjoy a nice solitary supper of grilled cheese and tomato soup, her favorite meal in the fall season, and get into bed to watch her nightly episode of *A Haunting* on the TV. She loved supernatural television shows, but Tom never let her watch them on the big screen downstairs (at least, not when he was home). They had a fifty-five-inch flat screen TV in the living room, but Tom made it a habit to sleep downstairs that year, so she had the TV upstairs and the bed all to herself, which was a blessing most of the time anyway.

Isobel heard Tom rustling about downstairs, and a couple of times she thought he was coming upstairs, but it was only him using the bathroom at the bottom of the steps that the sound of him moving would startle her. He never did come up to their bedroom that night and Isobel was actually able to get some sleep.

The following morning there was a loud knock on the front door. It made Isobel jump. No one ever used the brass knocker that hung on their door. Most people rang the doorbell. Tom had already left for work and Isobel was still in her night clothes when she answered the door to a man standing on her front porch holding a box. It was Arthur from the bazaar. She invited him in for a cup of coffee and some conversation because she had some questions for him about the typewriter she had purchased.

After sitting down at the kitchen table for a few minutes while Arthur took the machine out of the box to show it to her, Isobel got up the nerve to ask a couple of questions that she felt were avoided the previous day. First, she asked about the company name because Arthur's daughter's name was Clara, but the business name was *Annie's Odds 'n Ends*. After finding out that Annie was his wife, who died of a freak accident the previous year, Isobel did not ask any more questions about her, even though she was curious about how she died.

She did ask why he referred to the typewriter as "special". Arthur just made up some story (at least Isobel *thought* it was made up by his nervousness when he spoke about it) about how it belonged to Annie and had sentimental value, but Isobel could tell by his lack of eye contact with her that there was more to that story.

Arthur started pointing to the different parts of the 1940's Royal typewriter and explained to her that the machine had recently been completely refurbished. That was how he justified it being so expensive. He also gave her a business card that had their web address on it in case she ever needed any additional parts. He explained that they made it a point to keep those particular parts in stock.

Isobel knew the Royal would be too heavy for her

to carry upstairs to her bedroom, so she asked Arthur if he would take it up there for her. She had a small desk that sat in front of a window, where she would sit and write her journals (which Tom knew nothing about). It would be cool to start writing them with this new (old) typewriter. The only problem would be explaining it to her husband, but she had all day to figure out how she would do that.

After the Royal was all set up, Isobel walked Arthur downstairs and to the front door, thanking him for everything.

"It's no problem. Just take care of her," he said, again as if the machine were human.

"Oh, I will," Isobel reassured him.

Arthur turned to walk away and then slightly turned back toward her. "And be careful," he added.

Isobel wasn't sure what he meant by that, but she gave a slight wave of her hand and closed the door with a slight feeling of apprehension, which was short-lived because she became suddenly anxious to play with her new purchase.

3

Isobel was seated in her chair doing some practice typing on her new typewriter (she wasn't yet used to a keyboard so extravagant, with its keys so spread apart), so she never saw it coming, as the back of Tom's hand broadsided her from behind, and knocked her right off her chair. Lying on her side and holding the side of her throbbing face, she looked up at him as tears flooded her eyes from the sudden burst of pain inflicted upon her.

"What the *fuck* is that?" Tom asked as he pointed to the typewriter, breathing heavily through his nose like an angry gorilla.

Isobel tried to gain her composure enough to give him an answer that would not result in another beating, realizing that, no matter what she said at that point, he would continue to hurt her. She struggled to find her voice. "It's just a typewriter," she said as she shielded her face with an open right hand.

"No shit, Sherlock," Tom said sarcastically, "I mean, where the fuck did it come from?"

Not bothering to attempt to get to her feet because she knew he would just knock her back down, she hesitantly said, "I bought it at the bazaar," she continued to shield her face, "with my own money."

He leaned down and shook his fist in her face. He was so mad he was shaking. "I knew you went to that damned thing!" He yelled, "Did you think I didn't know?" He directed his attention to the Royal, reached over with both hands, and picked up the heavy writing tool. He threw it to the floor, causing several of its pieces to dislodge and scatter all around the room. "Clean this shit up!" He said with fury in his voice as he turned to exit the room. He got off on making messes just to have his wife clean them up.

After the door slammed behind him, Isobel started to cry as she put her hands over her eyes. She knew he would be mad and she knew she would get the snot beat out of her, but that didn't make it any easier to deal with. She scrambled to get to her feet without slipping on any of the small bits of typewriter around her. She stood up and went into the bathroom to check out the new wound that was appearing on her cheek, and to clean up her face before cleaning up the mess her husband created all over the floor.

Her right cheek was already starting to turn blue. She looked into the mirror and tried to decide how she would conceal this new bruise, which was developing over an older one that was faded to a yellowish green. She put a cold washcloth on it for a few minutes before using the same washcloth to wash her entire face. She then took some aspirin out of the medicine cabinet and popped two of them into her mouth, swallowing them without any water. She was so used to having to take pain medication that the need for a drink to wash pills down was something she no longer required. After blotting her face with a towel she kept on a small rack next to the sink, she walked back into her bedroom, hoping Tom had not returned.

Realizing he was nowhere in sight, Isobel noticed an unusual chill as she entered the bedroom, so she wrapped her arms around herself in an attempt to warm up. That was when she saw it. She could not believe her eyes. The Royal typewriter was back up on her table and the pieces appeared to all be intact. She thought, for a brief moment, that maybe Tom came in and fixed it while she was in the bathroom. She knew that was completely out of character for him, but it was the only explanation she could come up with.

As she crept downstairs she did not hear any sound coming from the first floor of the house. Usually she could hear Tom so she knew where he was. She liked to know where he was because he was someone you did not want to sneak up on. She knew what the consequences would be for that.

Once downstairs, she slowly moved toward the living room and then to the kitchen, finding both of those rooms empty. Tom was nowhere in sight. She even got up the nerve to knock lightly on the small half-bath downstairs, but she got no answer from the other side of the door. She opened it and did not find him. She wondered where he could be as she walked back toward the kitchen to get herself a glass of water.

Isobel stood at the kitchen sink sipping her ice water when she looked out the window over the sink.

There, she saw Tom. He was outside at the next-door neighbor's house talking with the cute blonde woman who lived there. Her name was Kim and she lived with her husband (who was never home) and their little dog Bentley, who was a cute little black and white cocker spaniel. Kimberly Maguire was a pretty woman who had long blonde hair and a slender body frame. She always looked nice, even when she was just outside working in her yard. Isobel envied this because she also liked to look nice but Tom wouldn't allow her to look decent because he didn't want other men looking at her.

She watched as Tom and Kim giggled and talked as if they were best friends. Isobel wished he would act that happy with her. Those days were gone a long time ago and she didn't remember exactly what had changed their relationship. They were so happy once, but it only lasted for the first couple of years of their marriage. They had been married now for over ten years, and Isobel felt like they were strangers most of the time.

Tom smiled at Kim and turned to go back home, so Isobel ran back upstairs so he wouldn't know she was watching him. She knew he wasn't the one who fixed the typewriter; he wouldn't do anything to help her. She went back to her room and just stared at the Royal, not really knowing what to think. The important thing was that it was cleaned up, and she was *not* going to ask Tom if he had anything to do with it. That was an answer she did not need and a backhand to her face that she did not want.

Isobel sat on the edge of her bed and looked away from the typewriter and down to the floor. She was shivering from the sudden change in temperature in her bedroom and she was confused as to what had just happened. She could not ignore the fact that the Royal, which now sat completely assembled on her table, was a scattered mess a few moments ago.

That Monday at the office, everyone was talking about the bazaar (well, the three people who worked there were). Isobel worked at a small real-estate company called Humphrey's Homes. She was never really a part of anyone's conversation as she always kept to herself. It wasn't just that Tom didn't like her hanging around other people; she was also paranoid someone would ask questions that she would not know how to answer regarding her appearance, the camouflaged one anyway. The lies she had to make up about falling down the steps or walking into doors were getting tiresome, and she knew no one believed them.

She was the receptionist for the company where only a handful of people ran the entire operation. She had a desk that was strategically placed immediately to the left of the front door so she could greet people as they walked into the office. There was a wide-open room inside the front door with a small hallway at the far end of it that led to a few offices. They were reserved for the real-estate agents.

The two agents working that Monday were Carissa and Carol; there was a third agent who worked there, but he was out of the office that day. Quinton had taken a paid week off to go to a real-estate conference in Las Vegas. The rest of the office found it was convenient that his work-related trip was in a city that a lot of people would die to go to for vacation. That seemed to be the way in their office. Whenever there was a trip that sounded more fun than businesslike, *he* got to go.

After settling into her morning routine, Isobel went over to the coffee station to make sure there was a fresh pot of coffee made and to get a cup for herself. Carissa came up behind her to get herself a hot cup, and she accidentally bumped into Isobel as she bent down to get the coffee filters from the cabinet. Isobel apologized and quietly went about her business of starting a fresh pot.

"No," Carissa said, "it was my fault." She noticed Isobel looking at the floor and it seemed like she was shielding her face with her hair. "Are you okay?"

Isobel turned away from her and with her back turned, she said, "I'm fine."

Carissa, knowing how private and reserved Isobel always was, didn't press any further, but she did notice the discoloration of Isobel's cheekbone before she quickly turned away, which she gossiped about with Carol when she thought Isobel couldn't hear her. Isobel's bruises and demeanor were often the talk of the office, but no one knew how to approach her about it.

Carissa Mattson lived locally, was married, and had a 14-year-old daughter named Chloe. She brought her into the office a lot when the kids were off from school due to all of the "professional" days that were listed on the school calendar. Most working parents wondered what exactly happened on all of those "professional" days. They seemed to have them a couple times a month.

Carol Patterson had a little bit of a commute to work because she lived in a town that was approximately forty-five minutes away. She also had a daughter, but Isobel was not sure exactly how old she was. She thought she was about the same age as Carissa's daughter, but she never saw her, except for in photos. Carol was divorced and didn't speak much of her ex-husband. She was seeing someone new, but no one knew who he was.

After answering a few phone calls and transferring them to the agents, Mr. Humphrey walked in the front door where a bell hung and 'ding, dinged' every time someone walked in the door. Mr. Humphrey always said he liked to know whenever someone walked in the door, and he trained his staff to listen for that jingling bell so they could greet all of their customers promptly.

He looked over at Isobel, "Good morning Ms. Parrish," he said.

Isobel wondered why he always called her that, never addressing her by her first name. She didn't mind because at least he was acknowledging her, which was more than most people did on any given day. Living with Tom had turned her into a loner.

Mr. Humphrey made his way through the office and said his good mornings before retiring to his own office, where he would surely be undisturbed for hours. He was a busy man running a very successful real-estate business.

Isobel sat and adequately did her job for the rest of that day, but she could not get her new typewriter out of her mind. She couldn't wait to get home and start using it, *really* using it. She didn't get a chance the previous day due to her husband's daily need to assault her. He worked late on Mondays so she knew she would have some privacy. Isobel's hours at the office were from eight to three, and it felt like forever that day but her three o'clock quitting time finally got there.

After seeing if her boss needed anything else, Isobel clocked out for the day and walked out the door, leaving the dangling bell dinging behind her. She never said goodbye to anyone else. She just got in her car, pulled out of the parking lot, and went home to play with her toy.

5

Tom was working at his construction site installing a cabinet into a new house (ironically, he built homes and his wife helped sell them) when he suddenly doubled over with the worst stomach cramp he had ever felt in his life. The sudden sharp pain felt like he had been kicked in the stomach as it brought him to his knees on the unfinished hardwood floor.

On his hands and knees for only two minutes or so, the pain started to subside as quickly as it happened. Tom was able to stand up, but when he started to make his way to a chair nearby, it happened again. The fierce, burning cramp (or whatever it was) made him stumble, and he almost fell. His coworker, Ron, came to his rescue and helped him get to the chair.

The chair was only a few feet away and by the time they made it there, he was completely out of breath. Ron made sure his ass landed on the seat and not on the floor as Tom let himself fall backwards in a game of *trust* between himself and the collapsible wooden chair.

"Are you okay man?" Ron asked.

Tom, barely able to get enough air into his lungs to speak, said, "Yeah, I must have picked up that stomach bug that's going around."

Ron asked him if he wanted a ride home, but Tom said he would be fine to drive in a few minutes. He wasn't usually one to leave work early and he was *never* sick, so this was a surprise to everyone.

Tom didn't understand where the weird pain came from, or what it was. He wasn't nauseous and he didn't have the shits, at least not *yet*. He just had severe, unexplained abdominal pain. His only thought was that it must have been something in his wife's cooking, which he would surely make her pay for when he got home, but for the moment, he just wanted to sit and collect his thoughts, and wait for the misery that was inside of him to go the hell away.

6

Isobel sat down at the table in her bedroom as soon as she got home (she sped all the way home and pulled up the driveway at 3:08) just as she planned. She had already decided she was going to write journal entries with the typewriter when she purchased it, probably just until she got comfortable with it. Then she might start to write things that were larger. Her only concern was figuring out a way to hide the papers. The journal she had already was one with a lock and key, so she would need a box or something she could store her papers in until she could sneak out to a store and get something more sufficient that would keep Tom out of it.

The first entry was about Tom. Actually, most of them were about him and the way he treated her. When she was not writing about him, she was writing about dreams of ways she would get away from him one day. She typed about the previous day's events when he beat the ever-loving shit out of her for going to the bazaar and buying something for herself. She would say things to her journal as if she was having a conversation with it and it could talk back to her.

After describing the torturous pain she felt when he knocked her to the floor, she typed a little scenario of her getting up and punching him in the stomach (something she had imagined doing on several occasions).

She knew she would never do that because, not only would it aggravate him more, but she was too small and weak compared to him. He would probably kill her if she ever did that. She just enjoyed writing about it because it made her feel better to describe Tom being the one in pain for a change and not being able to walk. She wanted to inflict some of her pain onto him, even though it was just words on paper. She typed about how he was in excruciating pain at his job and, for once, *he* was the one who was embarrassed, *not* her. *He* was the one who had to leave and had no good explanation as to why, *not* her.

In Isobel's story, Tom begged her for mercy as she continually kicked and punched him in the stomach. She kicked him in the face as he bent over and held onto his midsection. She gave him a bloody nose before she abruptly stopped typing.

Isobel looked down at the paper and could not believe those words came out of her. She was so angry and needed to be able to express her emotions like she had never been able to do before. She now had a way to do that and the idea of it was exhilarating.

After typing the bullshit story that actually did make her feel a little better, she yanked the paper out of the machine and crinkled it up. She looked out the window and thought, *who the hell am I kidding?* Then she dropped the paper into a trashcan next to her bed and sat on the edge of her bed and thought about starting a new journal entry.

When Isobel started typing again she left out the stuff about her beating upon her husband. She also talked about how excited she was to have the new type-writer because it gave her an outlet to vent. Lord knew she needed that. She felt, in a weird kind-of way, that she finally had something she could depend on that would not judge her. It was only a typewriter, but she felt a connection to it from the moment her fingers started typing on its keys.

7

Tom finally built the strength up to attempt the drive home. Lucky for him, it was only a short drive. When he got into his Ford pick-up, he did not even fasten his seatbelt because it hurt to pull it over his stomach. He started the truck and just the vibration of the engine made him ache. He slowly pulled out of the dirt driveway and started to head home.

He only made it about half a mile before he had to pull over. He was struck with a sudden force to his face. His nose felt like something hit him. He frantically looked around his truck for anything that could have hit him in the face, while at the same time, he struggled to get to the side of the road. He put his hand up to his nose to catch the blood that had started to drip down to his chin. Catching the blood with his right hand, he yanked the steering wheel to the right with his left hand (cutting several cars off in the process) and pulled over onto the shoulder of Route eighty-four.

Tom searched the glove box for some napkins or anything to wipe his face, but came up empty handed. Then he spotted an old white tee shirt behind his seat. He picked it up and cleaned his nose and face with it. After also wiping his hand (which was also covered with blood) he continued his drive home. The entire excursion turned his ten-minute drive into a thirty-minute one.

He finally arrived at his home just before four thirty, which was perfect because he knew his wife would not be expecting him until around six o'clock, maybe even seven. This would certainly surprise her and he could not wait to *talk* with her about what had happened to him.

Yeah, he would give her a talking to alright...

Tom parked his truck, got out, and slowly walked (hunched over) to the front door. He entered quietly and did not see Isobel anywhere downstairs. He headed to the staircase where he figured he would discreetly climb the stairs so Isobel would not hear him. However, the steps were a little difficult for him because every time he lifted one of his legs in the upward step motion, he felt a sharp, fierce pain shoot across his mid-section. He was able to fight through this, but it did slow him down.

He could see their bedroom door open at the top of the stairs. It was just to the left of the top of the steps. Knowing his wife had to be in there, he fought his way through the pain until he got about halfway up. Then he stopped suddenly, or he *was* stopped suddenly and it wasn't by his own doing (at least he didn't think so). He hit his head on something that was right in his way, at least he thought there was something there. He couldn't see anything, so he put his hand out in front of him, but it also was stopped in midair. Tom felt like he was losing his mind. He started to think that whatever his wife fed him was affecting his judgement and it was only pissing him off more.

Tom tried to continue, but it was like he was walking into an invisible wall. He was so unbelievably mad at that point, he yelled Isobel's name up the stairs but it didn't seem to make it up to her. The sound of his voice simply ricocheted off the invisible obstacle before him and flew back at him like a slap in the face completely throwing him off balance to the point he had to grab the railing with both hands to prevent himself from sailing down the steps. He had worked too hard to get to where he was on the staircase and was not about to let that happen.

"Bitch, you better hope I don't get up there!" He yelled, but he got the same response from the invisible force field.

Again, he struggled to hold onto the railing. His anger grew to the point he had to hit something and since Isobel was not in front of him, he started pounding his right fist on the invisible obstacle, while holding tightly to the banister with his left. "ISOBEL!!!", he screamed as his breathing became relentless.

Tom did not understand what was happening as the barrier continued to keep him from ascending the stairs any further. He had not heard a peep from his wife and, at that point, he could not even be sure she was up there.

He was about to give up, but decided to give it one last blow to see if he could punch through to the other side, when a strong, cold wind surfaced around him. For a moment he became frightened, which was short-lived when the invisible wall suddenly smashed, and blew him down the steps, where he landed on his back at the bottom of the staircase.

Unable to stand right away, Tom looked up at the place he had been standing on the steps, but there was nothing there. There was no glass on the floor, even though he heard it smash. It did not make sense. Something made a crashing sound and blew him to the floor. He stayed there for a minute before he attempted the agonizing effort to get back on his feet.

Tom had no idea what had just happened. All he knew was that he was in a lot of pain and he just got his ass kicked by something that was not there. He wasn't about to try to go back upstairs, so he went into the kitchen, got himself a six-pack of Yuengling (he could never drink just one or two beers) from the refrigerator, and went into the living room to sit on the sofa and plot his next move. He was having second thoughts about approaching Isobel after his invisible ass kicking, or his stomach ache because he thought it would only make him look crazy and it would give her some ammo against him. He certainly did *not* want that.

As he started to drink his first beer, which he knew would take away some of the pain he was feeling, he turned The History Channel on the TV because he could always count on that to get his mind back into the neutral zone (which didn't make any sense because the shows on that station were mostly about war and death). Something about the Battle of Gettysburg came on and Tom sat back, downed a couple of his beers and started to doze off.

He was able to catch about twenty minutes worth of Zs before he was awakened when the TV was shut off. He opened his eyes and saw the wife he loathed at that moment standing in front of him. He jerked his body upward in an attempt to get up from the sofa and grab her before she could go back upstairs, but he was stopped short by the sharp pain that was still haunting his abdominal cavity, and he could not stand up.

Isobel was surprised at her husband's struggle to get up off the sofa as he held onto her wrist. She had no idea what he had just been through (which was a shame because she surely would have enjoyed it). She liked to believe in karma, but it never seemed to help her out. She looked at Tom as he continued to try to move off the couch.

"Are you alright?" she asked as she tried to pull away from him.

"Am I *alright*" He mocked in his all-too-familiar sarcastic tone. "No, I'm *not* alright," he said, "and you won't be either once I get up from here!" His anger was prominent and Isobel hoped against hope that he would not get up.

Finally, able to break away from the robust grip of Tom's hand, Isobel quickly backed away from the sofa. She knew by the way he was acting that he would not be able to get up and catch her, although she did not know why. She had no idea what he had encountered on the stairs, nor did she care. She glanced over at the coffee table and noticed the three empty Yuengling bottles, and just assumed he took some kind of drunken stumble and hurt himself.

Tom was able to sit up, "Where were you?" he asked her, "I was calling your name."

Isobel knew she had to choose her words wisely, "I was in the shower," she said without looking him in the eye so he wouldn't be able to see the dishonesty in her. "I'm sorry. I didn't expect you home yet, but I will get dinner started."

Isobel figured getting his mind off her and refocusing it on dinner would put her in the clear so she would not get locked into a conversation that might lead to her divulging the truth, that she was typing an injurious story about him.

On Tuesday, Tom did not go to work. He did not want to have to explain his swollen face to anyone. Isobel decided to leave the house at seven, which was early for her, but she didn't want to have to deal with him. She made up a story about her office opening early for a mandatory meeting, but she actually stopped at Starbucks and treated herself to a grande iced hazelnut latte with an extra shot of espresso on her way to work to kill some time because she did not have to be at work, for *real*, until eight. The coffee also would boost her motivation for the day. After enjoying her iced morning caffeine, she continued her drive to the office in a somewhat better mood than usual.

Once she got to work, Isobel sat at her desk with a half-smile on her face, while she started her day by answering a few phone calls. Her coworkers gawked because a smile was something they were not used to seeing on Isobel's face. She answered phone calls in a cheery tone and even spoke to a few people at the coffee station when she took her mid-morning break (not that she needed any more coffee). Carol was one of the people who approached her and actually spoke to her.

"How's it going, Isobel?" Carol asked her.

"I'm good," she responded. "How about yourself?" She asked and Carol looked like she did not know what else to say to her.

"I'm okay," she said after a short pause. "You look good today," Carol said as she pointed out the nice red blouse Isobel was wearing.

Isobel looked down at herself. "Thanks," she said as she started to turn away.

"Hey, a few of us are ordering pizza for lunch today," Carol was quick to catch her before she went back to her desk. "Would you like to join us?"

Isobel looked back over her shoulder. She could not believe she was invited to have lunch with them. "Yes. That sounds great," she said as she turned away from Carol and looked at the floor. "Thanks for including me."

"Great," Carol said. "I will be placing the order around eleven thirty so the pizza gets here by twelve," she continued. "We are just going to eat it back here at the break table."

Isobel looked up hesitantly. "Just let me know how much I owe so I can help pay for it."

"Don't worry about it," Carol said. "This is my treat. We treat each other from time to time. You can get it another time."

That all sounded wonderful to Isobel. She went back to her desk and continued on with her morning routine, but she could not get her mind off lunch. She hoped she would be able to think of things to talk about with her coworkers because she was so used to being alone.

Lunch time arrived and Isobel enjoyed some pizza and some friendly conversation with her coworkers, Carol and Carissa, for the first time since she started working there. The conversation centered around funny happenings at the office, and what everyone was planning on doing after work and for the upcoming weekend. Although Isobel didn't add much to the conversation, she joined right in with the laughter and carrying on. She was glad she joined them because she got to know them a little and they got to know her, just a little.

Tom had slept on the couch because he did not want to try to venture upstairs after what happened the previous day. He was able to get himself up and make some coffee that morning, but he still felt some residual aching in his lower abdomen and his nose. Once he had his cup of coffee, he knew he needed to go upstairs in order to get ready for his day. He approached the steps with caution and paused at the bottom. He stared up at them and audibly chuckled to himself because he knew there couldn't be anything there to block him.

How crazy is this?

You're fine, you idiot! Just go up there.

There's nothing there, right?

As he continued to convince himself everything was going to be okay, he climbed the steps one at a time with one hand reaching out in front of him for any barriers that might be in his way, and his other hand firmly grasping the banister. When he reached the halfway point and nothing stopped him, he figured he was safe because that was where he met his invisible demon yesterday. Tom continued to the top of the stairs where he paused and let out an immense sigh of relief before continuing into the bedroom.

In the doorway to the bedroom he paused as he looked up and saw the typewriter by the window. There was no paper loaded into it, so he figured his wife was not using it.

She better not if she knows what's good for her!

He wanted that damned thing out of the house, but he decided to leave it alone at that point and just lie down on the bed. He still didn't feel that great and he had not gotten much sleep the night before because of his stomach pain. He would deal with his wife and her typewriter later.

He could not fall asleep right away due to the freakish happenings from yesterday circling around in his head. He was flat on his back with his head on his memory foam pillow for about thirty minutes before he finally drifted off to sleep.

Tom slept like a baby for a couple of hours once he finally fell asleep. His sleep was deep and soothing until he started to slowly come alive by the feeling of something prickly on his legs. Not knowing if he was dreaming or not, he rolled over onto his side to try to go back to sleep, but his eyes were trying to open and focus. The tickling sensation he felt on his legs drifted down to his feet and bothered him too much. He knew he had to get up.

Tom felt a sudden sharp sting in his calf as if he was stung by a bee. He sat up abruptly, ignoring the stomach pain he was still experiencing, and yanked the bed's comforter off himself to reveal his worst nightmare, a bed full of rats. Tom was not afraid of much, but he was *terrified* of rats and, to his horror, they were crawling all over him.

He panicked and started kicking his legs to get the rodents off him as he threw the comforter on the floor. He swung his legs off the side of the bed so he could get down, but the entire floor was crawling with the ferocious little beasts. Their beady red eyes stared up at him while their pink tails intertwined like earthworms as they stomped all over each other. The squeaking noises they all made in unison were unbearable so he covered his ears with the palms of his hands to try to block it out. It only got louder!

This can't be happening! WAKE UP YOU IDIOT!

"GET THE FUCK OUT OF HERE YOU LITTLE SHITS!" Tom screamed.

Then he moved his hands from his ears to his eyes to try to escape the horror. He sat still for a couple of minutes and he could feel the little sharp rat toes dig into his skin as they continued to run all over him and make a playground out of his bed. He knew the only way out of this nightmare would be to jump on the floor and run out of the room. So, to get himself ready to do that, he took a deep breath, closed his eyes tightly, and counted to three, out loud. Then he opened them to the shock and mystification that was on the other side of his eyelids. The room was empty and quiet. The rats were gone and all that was on the floor was the comforter that he had thrown there.

What the hell just happened, Tom thought as he looked around the empty room for any signs of them. He *knew* he saw (and felt) them. He looked at his legs and there were no marks, not even where he was sure he had been bitten. *Had it all just been a hallucination?*

The rat incident mixed with the unexplained stomach issue and what happened on the stairs all continued to make Tom think he was losing his mind. As he looked around his bedroom, the only things he saw were the bed, the table by the window, the chair, an empty trashcan, and the Royal typewriter.

Carol Patterson rushed home from work because she had a dinner date. She had been seeing Bill for a while now and he was taking her somewhere special for their six-month anniversary. She felt like a school girl around him. She got all giddy when she talked about him to anyone. However, he wasn't comfortable with a lot of people knowing they were seeing each other, so she rarely mentioned his name when she spoke of him. The only person who knew his name was her daughter Nikki.

He knew she had a 14-year-old daughter and he seemed to be okay with that. After her divorce, she had sworn off men and didn't think she would ever be in a relationship again, at least not for a long time.

Bill showed up at her house promptly at six, just like he said he would and Nikki answered the door. "Mom will be out in a minute," she very politely said to him before going back into the living room where she had been watching TV.

Bill never asked, but he figured Nikki didn't have too many friends. She was always home, unlike most girls her age who always wanted to be out. It wasn't cool to stay at home unless yours was the house where the "cool" parents lived, the ones who let the kids do whatever they wanted. There was always one of those in every neighborhood.

"Thank you." Bill said.

Bill thought Nikki was a real sweet girl (from what he knew of her), but he was not keen on the fact that her hair seemed to be a different color every time he saw her. He thought she was a little too young to be given the freedom to change her appearance so drastically all the time. She also wore dark, heavy make-up and dressed in black most of the time. She was cute and didn't need make-up, not to mention; a 14-year-old should not be wearing make-up anyway. Bill certainly had his opinions, but he didn't think it was his place to express them in the matter, so he just left it alone.

Carol came out of her bedroom looking all fresh, wearing a slender pink form-fitting dress that went down her thighs and stopped just above her knees. She had matching shoes on and her hair and make-up were like that of a supermodel in one of those runway magazines.

Bill looked at her with eyes that made her feel secure about the way she looked. He walked away from the front door where he had been waiting and met her at the end of the hallway, holding out his hand, "Shall we?" He asked.

Carol's cheeks turned a shade of pink that was so bright and shiny it shone through her make-up as she blushed, took his hand and said, "Absolutely, Mr. Mattson." She then directed her attention to her daughter. "Nikki, we won't be late," she said. "There are leftovers in the fridge for you to heat up for dinner."

Nikki did not look away from the television. "Okay, Mom," she said as she gave them a side wave to say goodbye.

Bill opened the door for her and led her to his Jeep Wrangler, where he also opened the door for her to get in. She loved his Jeep. It went along with his ruggedness, which she found attractive. He was also an auto mechanic, which was another plus as far as she was concerned. She liked a man who could fix things, (unlike her ex-husband who didn't know the difference between a screwdriver and a wrench).

Their date was at a quaint little restaurant near Carol's house in Hollow Creek called Carrie's Cuisine. They had appetizers, dinner, and dessert, which was a seven-layer chocolate cake with chocolate icing and vanilla ice cream. Carol was about to burst when they were finished. They sat for a while and finished a bottle of wine before Bill drove her home.

She was home by nine. Bill always had her home pretty early, and never came in for a night cap after any of their dates. Carol never pushed the subject. She was just happy she was dating someone who seemed to be so into her.

When Carol went into the house, Nikki was already in bed. It was a school night so she had to get up early in the morning. Nikki was so good about getting herself in bed and ready for school, even though she hated high school. The students picked on her because of the way she looked all the time. Carol peeked in on her before turning in herself to try to get a good night's sleep. She was never really able to sleep on the nights she and Bill went out because she could not stop thinking about him.

Isobel pulled up her driveway and parked her car. Before getting out, she took a deep breath because she did not know what kind of wrath would be waiting for her when she got into the house. At a slow pace, she exited her car and walked up to the front door where she took another deep breath.

Inside the house she did not see Tom anywhere. She checked every room downstairs before venturing to the second floor. She went into their bedroom, but still, nothing. She changed into some comfortable clothes (sweat pants of course), and she went into the bathroom to wash her face before finally getting up the nerve to holler Tom's name.

At first, she got no answer.

After her second call, his voice was heard muffled through the wall. "I'm in here," he said.

She was surprised to find him in their guest bedroom. She approached the door and lightly knocked. Oddly, he was nice and said she could come in. She opened the door and saw him lying on the bed,

"Are you feeling okay?" She asked.

"I'm fine," he snapped, "I'm hungry though."

She took the hint and closed the door and went downstairs to start dinner. She was just going to make spaghetti that night. She used sauce she had in a jar.

Tom preferred it when she made sauce from scratch but she figured out a way to just use a jar and add spices to it, along with some sliced tomatoes and mushrooms. He never knew the difference. However; she prayed she would never see the day when he found out what she was doing. He would most-likely beat her with the pot she used and throw the hot spaghetti at her. He liked to throw things during his tantrums.

After the water she had placed on the stove made its way to a rapid, rolling boil, Isobel prepared the sauce (well, the fake sauce that she would try to pass as her own), and began to slice a loaf of bread so she could make some garlic bread. It wasn't long before the entire house was filled with the aroma of baked garlic bread and the scents of Italian cooking. This was Tom's favorite meal and she did not want any fights this evening, so the meal was really, more for her than for him. She had just had a great day at work, for a change, and did not want Tom to ruin her mood.

Isobel opened the oven door and bent down to get the bread out because the timer had gone off, when Tom walked up behind her making her jump and almost drop the pan, bread and all. "Oh shit!" She gasped, "you scared me!"

"It smells good," he said as he opened the refrigerator and grabbed a Yuengling noticing there were only three left. "Looks like I have to make a beer run," he said and closed the door.

Isobel turned to look at him and noticed he looked

a little pale and he looked as though he had been sweating. She reached up to put her hand on his forehead to see if he had a fever or something, but he flinched away from her touch. Not wanting to push the subject, she turned back to the dinner that was cooking on the stove, stirred the sauce and drained the noodles into a strainer she had already placed into the sink.

Tom grabbed his keys and walked out the door without another word. She figured he was going to get his beer, so she decided to set the table and wait for him to come back so they could eat together, but all she wanted to do was go upstairs and type on the Royal. She didn't know why, but that typewriter was all she could think about since she got it home. She hoped her husband would plant himself in front of the TV after dinner like he normally did so she could type without being disturbed (or without him even knowing, for that matter).

Tom was only gone for a few minutes before he walked back in the front door with his six-pack and planted himself at the dinner table. He always expected Isobel to serve him and she did this without hesitation as to not get involved in an argument. She dished his spaghetti onto his plate and brought him a glass for his beer, which he didn't use because he drank it right out of the bottle.

They only sat at the table for about fifteen minutes because they were both anxious to get away from each other's company and go about their own business. When Tom was finished, Isobel took his plate to the sink for him and suggested he go into the living room to watch TV as she did the dishes. He did exactly that without any argument. He didn't fight with her when everything was going *his* way.

She piled all of the dishes on the counter and prepared the dishwater. They had a dishwasher, but her husband did not allow her to use it. He said it waisted too much power and a woman should be hand washing dishes anyway.

It only took her ten minutes to finish the dishes, and as she was draining the sink, she turned on the garbage disposal because she had lost a few noodles down the drain. The disposal was almost on its last leg and it shook the entire sink when it turned on. Soapy water splashed around when it was running. Isobel had asked Tom to get a new one, but he was always so concerned about money.

Isobel was just about to flick the switch to turn the garbage disposal off when it made a god-awful noise, and suddenly stopped on its own. It sounded like something was caught in the blades and she knew the only way to find out was to stick her hand down there. She made sure she turned the switch to the off position before beginning the slow journey with her hand down the drain to fix the problem. She was nervous as she felt around the bottom of the sink for a clog or something. She hesitated as her fingers slowly explored every piece of debris and machinery until she found it. There was something lodged in there that she could not see, but it felt like a piece of metal.

She pulled her hand out of the drain and put a rubber glove on, and then proceeded to guide her hand back down to the spot where she thought she felt the culprit. She found it and realized it was round and felt like a little toy or something. She got ahold of it with her index finger and thumb and tugged. She did not have to pull real hard, as the item easily dislodged itself from the mechanism and came out in her hand.

Isobel got it close enough to where she could see it, and she could not believe her eyes. It was a small round plate with the letter 'K' on it and she quickly recognized it as one of the keys from her new typewriter, or at least it looked pretty darn close. She grabbed a dish towel and wiped it clean, peeked in on Tom to make sure he was still watching TV, and she ran upstairs with the 'K' in her hand. She made it to their bedroom and it only took a second for her suspicion to be confirmed. The key was missing from the Royal's keyboard. She placed the letter on the table next to the Royal and left the room.

The alarm woke Isobel up at nine in the morning and she got out of bed and glanced at her typewriter. She had not used it the previous night due to the broken key. It was her day off so she got dressed in jeans and a sweatshirt and went downstairs to make some coffee. She figured Tom was already gone for the day (he had stopped kissing her goodbye a long time ago). She realized she was mistaken when she went to the sink to get water for her coffee pot and looked out the window. Tom was in the side yard talking with Kim, the neighbor who Isobel was sure he had a crush on. She turned away to finish making coffee and get started with her day, but she did wonder why Tom hadn't left for work yet.

After grabbing an apple for herself for breakfast, Isobel could not help but to look out the window again and the view did not change. Tom was smiling at Kim as she talked to him about something that was probably so unimportant, and that he most-likely could not hear a word of due to his obvious juvenile crush on the woman.

As she bit into her apple and continued to watch them, she could not help but remember a time when Tom looked at *her* like that. He would smile at her touch and the sound of her voice as he hung on her every word. It was the way newlyweds acted for the first couple of years of their marriage, but for Tom and Isobel, it ended when they got married. Isobel suffered her first beating on their honeymoon in Bermuda after a fabulous day of sailing and walking on the beach. Tom was so jealous because he noticed some men checking out his new wife in her skimpy bikini. Isobel thought it would just be a one-time thing and it wouldn't happen again. And it *didn't* happen again for a long time, but it *did* happen. It was also a couple of years later when he made her start dressing differently so she would not look so attractive to other men.

Tom kept smiling at Kim in a way that made Isobel nauseous. He said something to her before turning to come back into the house. Isobel sat at the dining room table eating her apple and pretending she didn't see anything. He did not say a word to her as he walked past her and went upstairs to get in the shower.

While Tom was in the shower, Isobel took the opportunity to go upstairs and try to fix her typewriter. She went into her bedroom and, to her surprise, the key was no longer sitting next to the typewriter where she left it. She looked on the floor and all around the area, but she didn't see it anywhere. She sat down on the chair in front of the writing table and noticed the keyboard looked normal. She looked closer (specifically, where the 'k' would be) and it was there. The key was intact as if nothing ever happened. The only explanation she could come up with was that Tom must have found it and put it back in place. But, why would he do that? He hated that typewriter.

Tom got out of the shower, put some clothes on and left for work without talking to her. She figured he was just going to work late. Whatever; she was just glad he was gone temporarily.

With Tom out of the house, Isobel was finally able to sit and enjoy her typewriter. She began to type and the words just came out of her mind, through her fingers, and onto the sheet of paper without so much as a second thought. It was like she was not in control of her hands as the Royal took over.

The typing continued for over an hour as Isobel stared blankly at the sheet of paper. She finally snapped out of her trance-like state, but not before she typed five pages she had no recollection of typing. She pulled the last sheet out of the machine and put it on the table with the other four she had apparently put there, before she got up and looked at what she had done. She could not believe there were five sheets of paper typed. Freaked out, she left the room without reading it and went downstairs to get a glass of water and try to make sense of what just happened.

13

Isobel was awakened by the sudden forceful shake of her husband's hand. He was shaking her shoulder trying to wake her up. She had apparently fallen asleep on the couch and the sun was going down. When she started to come to, she realized she must have been sleeping for hours. Tom was back from work and it was almost dusk.

"Isobel!" Tom hollered. "What is going on?"

Isobel rubbed her eyes and was awakened further by the flashing red and blue lights that were beaming in through the windows from all directions.

She looked at Tom, "Where is that coming from?" she asked.

"Next door," he said, "at Kim's house." He ran to the window to get a better look.

"I must have fallen asleep," Isobel said, "I don't know what's going on."

"I hope everything is okay," he said, and went outside to check it out for himself.

There was an ambulance and a police car in the driveway of their neighbor's house. Almost as soon as Tom got outside, two paramedics wheeled a stretcher out of the house next door. Tom ran over to see if it was Kim. They had her face covered, but her blonde hair hung over the side of the stretcher giving her identity away. Tom tried to get close to her, but he was stopped by a police officer.

"Sir," the officer said. "Please stay back."

"What happened?"

"We cannot disclose any information at this time," the officer said.

"Is she alright?" Tom asked.

"We are not sure," the officer said. "She had an accident. When was the last time you saw Ms. Maquire?"

"This morning," Tom said, "before I left for work."

"We are just trying to see if anyone was with her at the time of her accident."

"What accident?" Tom almost yelled.

"Ms. Maquire burnt herself with hot water," the officer said. "Right now, it looks like she was alone at the time."

That was all he was going to say. The officer walked over to the paramedics, had a brief conversation with them, and got into his cruiser. Both vehicles drove away with their lights on and their sirens blaring, leaving Tom in his front yard to wonder how badly Kim was hurt and what had happened.

Isobel just looked out of her window wondering if Tom would be so worried if it had been her. Realizing she already knew the answer to that question, she walked away from the window and went upstairs to get ready for bed. She thought she would do a little reading before bed to clear her mind.

In her room, she put some pajamas on, brushed her

hair out, and went over to her bed to look for the book she was currently reading, *The Kept Woman*, by Karin Slaughter. She reached for it on her nightstand and glanced at the table with the papers on it that she had typed earlier. Curious, she grabbed the sheets of paper, propped her pillow up behind her back on her bed, and began to read that instead.

Tom went to the hospital to see how Kim was and to try to find out what happened to her. He arrived at the emergency room where the receptionist, who looked like she hated her job, looked down her nose at her computer screen, and did not even acknowledge Tom standing in front of her, though she must have known he was there by his impatient tapping on the counter.

After a few seconds he said, "Excuse me. I am looking for a friend of mine."

Without even looking up at him she continued to type and said, "Name?" Tom wondered what she was typing because he hadn't given her any information yet.

"Kim Maquire," he said as he looked around the waiting room at all of the sickly people who appeared to have been there for a while. Some of them were sleeping; others were too busy coughing and making awful hacking noises. There was one woman in the corner puking into a basin, the kind they give you at the hospital that is too small to vomit into if you have anything of substance in your stomach.

"It looks like she is in room five," the woman finally said. "But you can't go in yet. She is with the doctor." The woman continued clicking the keys on her keyboard. "Next?" She hollered over Tom's shoulder.

Tom, not wanting to infect himself, walked back toward the door where he stood and waited for almost an hour. He finally went back over to *Ms. I Love My Job*, and asked how much longer it would be. She looked at her computer and did some more of that annoying typing for a minute before saying she would have him buzzed right in. She picked up her phone to ask someone in the back to open the door.

Tom heard a loud buzzing noise to his right and watched as the electronic door opened all by itself. He did not waste any time. He quickly went through the door and started looking for room five. It wasn't hard to find. The rooms were numbered in order. Kim's was the fifth room on the right, just past the restroom.

Kim was lying flat on her back on the hospital bed. Her face was wrapped in bandages and Tom could hear her crying. He slowly walked over to the side of the bed.

"How are you?" he asked. "I'm sorry to just show up like this, but I was worried and noticed John wasn't home." John was her husband who, Tom assumed, was at work.

"How does it look like I am?" Kim asked as she fought back tears. "I was so stupid. I shouldn't have carried the teapot across the room." She just kept talking and Tom let her. "Why didn't I pour the tea at the counter where I always do? Why was I so stupid?"

As Kim continued to talk, Tom was getting information as to what happened to her. He did not know yet exactly what happened, but Kim was indirectly filling him in.

"I am here if you need anything," Tom said. That was the only reply he could think of to say.

"You can't help me!" she snapped at him. "They say I have third degree burns over fifty percent of my face!" She was almost yelling at this point and a nurse came in the room and told Tom it was time for him to leave.

Tom walked out of the room while Kim continued to rant about her face and how mad she was at herself. He did not get to see her face since it was all wrapped up when he was there, but he knew it had to be bad.

As he drove home, he wondered if anyone had called her husband to let him know what happened because he was nowhere in sight at the hospital. Tom thought if John Maquire was home once in a while, Kim's accident might not have happened. Tom despised John and he barely even knew him.

Sitting up comfortably in her bed, Isobel began to read the first page she had typed. Ironically, the story began with a woman named Kim, just like her neighbor. The pages were in a story format like she had written a short story. She was still amazed that she did not remember writing the words on the paper, but considering everything her husband put her through on a daily basis, it was surprising she even remembered to brush her teeth most days. She was quite scatter-brained most of the time.

The first page was simply about a woman named Kim who was always home alone because her husband worked so much (just like her neighbors). One night while he was at work she decided to make herself a cup of hot tea. She went into the kitchen, put water in the teapot and turned the burner on. She waited until the pot whistled like a steam engine before turning off the stove. Isobel wondered why she had written such a boring story, at least it seemed to capture the monotony of everyday life.

Isobel thought the narrative seemed kind of weird and she was about to just throw it in the trashcan when it suddenly became more interesting. Kim, the main character, picked up the teapot and carried it over to her table where she left her tea cup. Just before she reached the table, she dropped the hot teapot on the floor causing boiling water to splash straight up through the top of the spout like a geyser, and splatter all over her face. She screamed, ran to the sink to put some cool water on her face, and called 911, as she could already feel the skin start to harden and blister.

Isobel looked up from the pages as a chill ran through her body. She did not know what happened next door, but there was someone taken away in an ambulance and then her husband disappeared. She wasn't sure, but something may have happened to Kim and that made the story in front of her kind of eerie. Nervous, but intrigued, she continued to read.

Her Kim (the one in the story she typed), was taken to the hospital by an ambulance after the 911 call. Before they loaded her on the stretcher, the paramedics put some kind of medical cream on her face and covered it up with gauze. Immediately upon their arrival at the hospital, she was taken into a room in the emergency department where a doctor came in to attend to her right away.

As the doctor took the gauze off her face, one nurse held Kim's hand while the other one assisted the doctor by placing the contaminated pieces of gauze onto a silver tray and disposing them into a trashcan marked 'Biohazard'. Kim saw the looks on their faces as her injuries were revealed. It's easy to know something is bad when your doctor's face looks like that. Kim saw that look and began to scream. The nurses held her down while the doctor sedated her with an injection of some sort of clear liquid that made her start to calm down immediately, and that was the end of page one of Isobel's story.

Isobel took a deep breath and set the first page face down on the bed next to her and daringly continued on to page two. As she continued to read, the doctor kept assessing and diagnosing his patient's face. He determined that the majority of Kim's burns were third degree and he started to plot a course of treatment with the nurses, while he called a second doctor to help him. He took photographs in case they had a domestic case in front of them. Kim had not had a chance to speak with them yet to tell them what happened.

The first thing the second doctor, Dr. Webster, did was get a kit ready for cleaning and debriding the burnt areas while the first doctor got his nurse to start her on IV fluids. Kim slept through this entire passage in the story due to whatever it was they sedated her with.

With the utensils needed to clean and debride Kim's face, the two doctors got to work. They worked hand in hand for over an hour trying to remove as much damaged skin as possible without going underneath the skin and into the soft tissues of her face. The goal was to ensure the least amount of permanent damage to Kim's face as possible, but with the severity of the burns, they knew the incident was going to leave their patient scarred for the rest of her life. The burnt areas were too big and the skin was so seriously damaged. There was only so much they could do before they put their tools away. They would have to figure out the kindest way to tell their patient she would have to live with the disfigurement.

It was about an hour after the doctors finished working on Kim when she started to show signs of life again. There was a nurse in the room checking on the fluid level of her IV bag when Kim started to make some grumbling sounds. After she made sure she did not need a new bag of IV fluids (which were a combination of some nutrients mixed with medications to try to avoid infection), the nurse went to get Dr. Webster to inform him that his patient was waking up. He immediately sent her back into the room with a syringe full of Dilaudid so Kim's pain would be minimal when she woke up. The nurse injected the morphine right into Kim's IV line and she immediately stopped making noise as her head fell gently to one side. The nurse just figured she drifted back into a deep sleep.

It was at that point Isobel had finished the second page and she began to feel a chill in the air in her bedroom. She didn't understand where it was coming from because her window was closed and it wasn't cold outside. She felt a slight breeze drift over her while she sat up against the headboard of her bed. She got up to retrieved a sweater out of her closet, pulled the comforter down on her bed so she could cover her legs with it when she climbed back onto the bed where she started page three.

Another nurse came into Kim's room where Kim laid like a corpse in the hospital bed. She took one look at the patient in front of her and gasped.

"What happened to this one?" she asked the other nurse that was in the room.

Nurse one said, "She burned her face with hot water," she was checking her vitals, "third degree burns," she said, "such a shame. She looks like she was pretty before this."

"Has she seen how bad it is yet?" Nurse two asked.

"No," Nurse one said, "she was just brought in and we started working on her right away. I don't want to be the one to give her a mirror for the first time."

Nurse two shook her head back and forth, "It's just horrible."

The nurses spoke freely in the room while their patient lay there lifeless, but able to hear them. Her body was having the luxury of not feeling anything, but her senses (like hearing and sight), worked just fine. Kim heard the conversation, but could not fully comprehend it due to the morphine that was making her high as a kite.

Dr. Webster came into the room. "Are you two doing your shift change?" he asked.

Nurse one looked at him, "Yes," she said, "I was just filling Nancy in on this patient's status."

"Ok, well I need someone in room two," he said. "The patient needs some sutures."

Both of the nurses walked out of Kim's room and

the doctor looked at her face. He put some more of the medical cream on her. She could feel its coolness seep into her skin. She slowly opened her eyes and looked blankly at the doctor who she was depending on to fix her face. He saw the fear in her eyes and grabbed her hand.

Kim slowly regained a form of consciousness that might not be classified as cognizant, but she wanted so desperately to speak with the doctor. She looked up at him, squeezed his hand tightly, and said with one small breath, "mirror."

He knew what she said, but he did not think she was ready for that yet. "Are you thirsty?" he asked to try to change the subject.

"No," she said, "mirror..."

It was clearer the second time so he could not pretend he didn't understand what she said. "Okay, I'll get one," he said, "but you have to understand what happened here and that we are not finished treating your injuries yet, not by a long shot."

With that said, he pulled a mirror out of one of the drawers that was in her patient room. He told her to let him hold it because she was weak from the medications. She agreed and Dr. Webster slowly moved the mirror in front of her face and that was the end of page three.

Isobel put the paper down with the others she had read and she noticed that her hands were now freezing. She could also hear the wind picking up outside. She got up from her bed and opened her window slightly to feel the temperature outside. It was fairly warm, but the wind was really starting to howl. She closed the window and decided there must be a storm coming in. That might explain the temperature change. As she tried to justify this in her head she knew it was not true. If that was the case it would be cold outside, but it wasn't. She just wanted to get back to her reading.

Isobel did not know why she typed the story she was reading or where the idea came from, but she was really getting into it. To make herself more comfortable, in addition to the blanket and sweater she was already using for warmth, she grabbed a pair of thick wool cabin socks out of her top drawer of her dresser because her feet were freezing.

She got under the comforter on her bed and picked up page four where she delved right back into the story of Kim, who was just about to look in the mirror for the first time since her accident.

Kim looked in the mirror and was horrified at the mutant that stared back at her that had now *become* her. She threw her hands over her mouth and gasped with panic. Tears instantly flooded her eyes and she grabbed the mirror out of Dr. Webster's hand so she could get a better look at herself.

The first thing she inspected was her nose, or what *used* to be her nose. The surface of the bridge of her nose was a deep maroon color with tiny blisters all over it. The left side of her nose had become a red, bubbly, skin flap that looked like it was puss-filled. Kim slowly and gently put her finger up to her skin and there was an immediate sensation of burning that ran down to her nostrils. She quickly yanked her hand away. The pain on the surface of her face was so great she could not even touch it. She wondered how the doctor planned on fixing it when she couldn't even handle the slightest touch.

Kim focused on her forehead and saw more of the same red, blistering skin, but the skin was peeling away right along her hairline. The surface of her skin was smooth and shiny. She wondered if her freckles were hiding under the burnt areas, or if they were gone for good. She kind of liked her freckles so she hoped she would get them back.

Her right cheek had a small area of redness right below her eye, but her left cheek was a different story. There were three or four large enflamed areas that were a deep red color. Two of them were blistered and the skin was broken. It looked like she had some kind of skin disease, like shingles. That pattern carried down to her chin as well. She was frightened at what she saw in those areas more than the rest of her face.

After a few minutes, Dr. Webster reached for the mirror, which Kim willingly gave to him.

"I'm not going to lie. It's bad," he said. "But I can fix it to a point."

Kim didn't say anything. She just continued to cry and rolled over so she was facing away from the doctor. It was as if she were mad at him.

Dr. Webster knew she didn't want to talk. "Get some rest and we will talk in the morning," he said, "I'm giving you a sedative in your IV so you can sleep."

Kim did not say a word. She drifted off to sleep as the new medicine ran into her bloodstream and that was the end of page four.

17

Isobel noticed the thick raindrops smacking against her bedroom window. They were making such a racket she got up to look outside. She could see the thick cloud cover that hovered over her neighborhood and the ricocheting lightning bolts throughout the night sky.

She opened her window slightly to hear the soothing sound of the storm because the sound of rain was relaxing for her. The wind instantly funneled in her window and the whirlpool of air surrounded her and held her like an invisible hug that would never let her go. Isobel found this to be a little eerie, but it only lasted a few seconds before the window slammed shut so hard she thought it might break. She checked the area around the window and nothing seemed to be disturbed, until she examined the typewriter that sat on the table just inside the window.

A couple of levers inside the Royal were moving and hitting the iron platen bar so hard they made a clapping sound which startled Isobel. Not wanting any damage to be done to the machine, she put a single sheet of white paper into the paper feeder and rolled it onto the bar so the letter levers would have a place to instill their ink. As soon as the paper was in place, the keys stopped moving and the lights went out throughout the house. Isobel knew it had to be due to the storm with its fierce lightning and loud crashing thunder she was beginning to hear.

Not wanting to stop reading when she was almost finished with her story, she lit a candle she kept on the table next to the typewriter. Briefly, she wondered where her husband was, but she was glad he was not home. His ruthless beatings were becoming more than she could take, and they were happening more frequently. She had been able to have a peaceful night without him being home.

Isobel got back into bed, and moved the first four pages of the story she did not remember writing aside, and picked up page five.

There was a knock at the door and Kim rushed out of her comfortable recliner to answer it. She wasn't surprised to see Tom standing on her front porch as she was expecting him. She opened it without hesitation. At that point, Isobel's suspicion was confirmed; the story *was* about her neighbor. He did not say a word. He stepped inside her door and grabbed her around the waist with such passion as he planted an intense open-mouth kiss on her lips.

"I thought you would never get here," she said, "I've missed you."

Tom looked into her eyes. "You know it's hard to get away from her sometimes. I thought she would *never* go to bed." He kissed her again on her lips as they made their way into her living room, wrapped in each other's arms. "Speaking of which," Tom continued. "Where is Johnny Boy?" he said sarcastically.

"Where do you think? Working," she said, "at least that's what he tells me. I'm pretty sure he is having an affair."

Tom pulled back from her, "Does that bother you?" he asked, "I mean, isn't that what we're doing?"

She giggled in her schoolgirl way, "Yeah, I guess so."

They continued to kiss while blindly taking off each

other's clothes on her sofa. They knew they wouldn't be disturbed by either one of their spouses.

"You are so beautiful and sexy," Tom breathed into her ear as his lips moved down her neck and toward her breasts.

Kim's heavy breathing turned into light moans of pleasure. She looked up at the ceiling while Tom continued to undress her down to her panties. She groaned and arched her back, but then felt a sharp pain shoot up her neckline which caused a sudden jolt in her and she sat up.

Kim opened her eyes to a room full of machinery and tubes hooked into her arm and realized it had all been a dream, a memory of a moment that had really happened and she knew would never happen again; not now, not with her monstrous face. It only took a few seconds and Kim was back to reality. Her affair with Tom was going to end and her husband would probably leave her for sure now. She started sobbing as she began to experience pain underneath the surface of the skin on her face.

Kim pressed the button to summon the nurse on duty to get some pain medication and to see if Dr. Webster was around. She had some questions for him after having time to think about her melted face, despite sleeping for most of the time.

Nancy, the nurse that took over her care at shift change, rushed into her room to see if everything was okay. "Is there something I can do for you?" she asked.

Kim's breathing was labored as she spoke, "Can I get something for pain?" she asked, "also, Is Dr. Webster around?"

"He got called into surgery," Nancy said, "and he will be there for a couple more hours. Is there anything else I can help you with?"

"No," Kim said, "I just have some questions for him."

"I will let him know when he is finished with his case," she said and she walked out of the room to get Kim some pain medication. Dr. Webster had written orders for Dilaudid to be administered as often as Kim needed it. Nancy returned with a new syringe of it and injected it into Kim's IV line. Again, she drifted off to sleep and that was the end of the story.

A lightning bolt shot across the sky and lit up Isobel's bedroom right before the thunder crashed like a sonic boom knocking the candle off her table, and leaving Isobel in complete darkness with her thoughts.

Isobel didn't hear Tom come in because of all of the noise the storm was making. All she knew was that when she knelt to feel around on the floor on her hands and knees for the candle, she was startled to feel her husband's boot instead. Isobel shrieked and jumped up so quickly she bumped her head on the table where her typewriter sat.

"I didn't hear you come in," she said as she slowly backed away from him, "I was just getting ready for bed." She lied because she did not want to answer any questions about what she was really doing.

The story she was just reading, she was sure now, was about her husband and the neighbor, and she knew it was probably a true story. If he found out that she knew, he would most-likely turn everything around to make it her fault so he could justify the beating he would give her. She lived with him long enough to know how these things played out. No matter the situation, it was always her fault and she had the marks on her body to prove it.

"What are you doing on the floor?"

"I tripped in the dark."

"Well," he said "Why is the power out anyway?" He snapped at her like it was her fault. "I work so damned hard woman! I paid the bill, so what did you do?" He asked as he shoved his finger in her shadow of a face.

Isobel backed farther away. "The storm knocked it out," she said as she backed away toward the bedroom door. "I didn't do anything, Tom."

That was all it took and he reached through the darkness for her until he was able to grab her arm. He pulled her back in the bedroom and threw her down on the floor. She struggled to get back to her feet, but before she was able to get up, he stomped on her back and knocked her back down. She fell face down on the carpet and did not make another attempt to get up. She just started to cry.

"What's the matter?" he barked, "Get up and find a candle or something, Woman!"

Isobel crawled away from him before getting back up to her feet. She remembered the candle she had earlier, the one that fell on the floor. She felt her way over to the table and found it, and grabbed a match out of the box she had put there earlier. She lit the wick and the flame lit up the Royal typewriter with the single sheet of paper in it. Isobel stared at it for a few seconds as the wheels in her head started to turn and an evil smile widened across her face, but then her attention was diverted back to her husband. She was working up the nerve to ask him where he had been all night when, to her surprise, he began speaking, unprompted.

Tom did not look at Isobel when he spoke, but she assumed he was talking to her. He went into a ten-minute ramble about how Kim had seriously burned her face with steaming hot water. Isobel stood silent and let him speak while her mind wandered in another direction. She hoped he would stop talking soon so she could just go to bed.

When Tom's discussion with himself finally came to an end, he walked out of the room without even looking at her.

Isobel let him leave while she worked up a plan in her mind to figure out if Kim's accident was related to the story she typed on the typewriter. That particular thought kept her awake for a while in her bed. *Had she, in some unconscious way, known what was going to happen to Kim? How could she?* Isobel's mind was a race track where no one was winning, before it finally settled down enough to let her fall asleep. It was just after midnight.

Isobel walked into Humphrey's Homes and went straight to her desk, where she knew she would have the freedom to get on the internet.

She wheeled her chair up to her desk, turned her computer on and directed the pointer on her screen to the Google icon. After launching Google, Isobel typed 'Annie's Odd's 'n' Ends' into the search bar and clicked 'search'. The tiny mom and pop store was not hard to find as it was the only one of its kind. The link appeared at the top of the listings and with one click of her mouse, Isobel was inside their website.

The motive was simple. Find a phone number, and call them. She found the number right away, but she had no idea what she was going to say when they answered the phone, but she knew she had to call.

Isobel dialed the number and after the phone rang four times, a man answered.

"Annie's," he said.

Isobel swallowed a large lump in the back of her throat and took a deep breath before she spoke. "Hello. I was wondering if Clara was around today." Isobel spoke as if she had not only met the girl once.

"Clara?" the gentleman asked. "She's not here." He coughed into the phone and cleared his throat before continuing. "She's with her dad at the fair in Green Acres."

That sparked Isobel's interest because Green Acres was only a thirty-minute drive from Humphrey's Homes. "How long will they be there, Sir?"

"That fair runs all week," he said. "Won't be back until Sunday night."

She could feel her heart start to beat faster. "Thank you so much," she said before abruptly hanging up the phone. She knew what she had to do.

Mr. Humphrey walked in the door as soon as she got off the phone and she immediately stood up and asked him if she could talk to him about something. He said yes and they went into his office where she made up a story about her husband being real sick and she felt the need to be with him. She knew that Mr. Humphrey thought she was nuts because Tom did not deserve her affection, not with the way he treated her, but he agreed to let her go home anyway.

Isobel packed up her things, thanked her boss and walked out the door where Carissa was walking in.

"Is everything okay?" Carissa asked noticing the way Isobel rushed past her to get out the door.

Isobel looked back at Carissa, "Yes," she said, "everything is just fine. I am leaving because Tom is sick and you know how men are," she giggled a little, "they are such babies when they get sick."

"Yeah, I guess they are," Carissa said, "I guess I'll see you tomorrow."

Isobel just nodded in agreement and continued to her car. She did not waste any time before she started it up and headed out of the parking lot. She knew how to get to Green Acres, but had no idea where they held their annual fair. She would just have to ask someone when she got there.

Her office happened to be on the main highway that led straight to her destination so the drive was easy, just a straight shot and she was there. She got there so quickly her Eagles CD didn't have time to play in its entirety (she also may have been slightly speeding).

Isobel pulled her compact car into the parking lot of the first convenience store she saw when she entered Green Acres territory, a Wawa, which happened to be one of her favorite places to get a sandwich. She went inside and asked the middle-aged, tattoo-ridden cashier if she could direct her to the fair. When the woman pointed out the window and told her which way to go, Isobel noticed the gaps in the front of her mouth where teeth used to be.

Satisfied with the directions and knowing she only had to make one more turn, Isobel left the store and continued her journey. She only had one more traffic light to pass before turning left. The cashier at Wawa said she would see lots of people and cars as soon as she tuned onto the main strip in Green Acres, and she wasn't lying. Isobel started to see a lot of people on foot as soon as she got to the light at Broad Street, the street the fair was on.

She decided to park her car at an Acme on the corner. She knew there would not be any place to park once she got closer to the fair. She could tell how crowded the event was just by the amount of people who were on foot heading into the fair.

Green Acres was a small town so the fair was not as large as the one back in Clairemont. It had a lot of the same features, like the clown with the balloons, the fair food aromas (cotton candy, popcorn, hot dogs, etc.), and the vendors. There was a fairly large crowd and Isobel figured the town's entire population must have been there, or people came in from different cities to check out the festivities. She knew the Clairemont fair had drawn in crowds from other places.

When she reached the festival, she looked at her watch as she was walking past the hot dog stand, where a young, attractive couple was selling hot dogs with all the fixings. They had the normal mustard, ketchup, and relish, but they also offered chili and cheese for the healthier appetite, which was the way Tom liked them. Isobel didn't care for all that mess on her hot dogs.

Realizing it was getting close to lunch time, Isobel decided to get a hot dog. The line was short and as she dug in her purse for some money to pay the vendor, she didn't realize the person in front of her was finished with his order and it was her turn.

"What can I get for you?" asked the cute blonde lady. She was very pleasant in her mannerisms. "We have a special today that includes a hot dog with chili, a bag of chips and a drink for five dollars."

Isobel looked up at her, still digging for her wallet. "I'll just have a hot dog with mustard," she said as her hand finally met with her change purse at the bottom of her handbag, where she knew she had some dollar bills.

"That will be three dollars," the woman said, "and the mustard is right over here." She pointed to a small table that was set up right next to their stand.

She handed Isobel the hot dog and Isobel handed her the money to pay for it. She thanked her, took the hot dog, put mustard on it, and looked around to see if she could see where Annie's Odds n' Ends was set up.

She spotted her target almost immediately as they were only two vendors away from the hot dog stand. As she eyeballed their set-up, she noticed that she did not see Clara anywhere.

When she headed toward the merchant, she stopped at a stand right next to them where an older woman was selling afghans, like the ones that were sold at her home bazaar. As she perused through the blankets she heard a soft voice behind her that could only belong to a child.

"Excuse me ma'am," the voice said.

Isobel turned around and was surprised to see the wheelchair. It was Clara. She was trying to get around Isobel in her chair (undoubtedly, to get back to her father), and she didn't seem to recognize her. Isobel stepped aside and let the girl pass, all the while wanting to scream out to get her attention.

Clara got about five feet away from her before she found the nerve deep within her stomach to say something. "Clara?" Isobel almost yelled.

The chair immediately turned around and the young girl looked at Isobel, obviously not remembering her. "Yes," Clara hesitantly said, "Do I know you?"

"I met you at the fair in Clairemont last week," Isobel said, "I bought that old typewriter from your dad."

Clara started to push herself in her chair to get around Isobel. "I'm sorry," she said without looking at her. "I have to get back." She wheeled herself past Isobel and toward her father's stand.

Not knowing what to say, Isobel hollered, "Wait!!" The girl did not turn around, so Isobel chased after her until she reached the back of her chair. She was about to grab onto the handles that stuck out the back, but chose not to before continuing, "I said wait. I want to talk to you about the typewriter I bought."

Clara looked back at her, "If there is a problem, you can talk to my father about it."

"No," Isobel quickly interrupted her, "I want to talk to you because you told me you had an issue with that machine."

She waited for a response for a long agonizing minute before Clara finally spoke. "We can talk, but not here."

"Fine," Isobel said, "wherever we need to go," she looked around to see if anyone was watching them, "I just have to talk to you about some things that have been happening."

"Give me a minute. Let me tell my dad I have to go to the bathroom so he doesn't get worried," she said, before wheeling herself away and chatting with her father for a few minutes.

While Isobel waited for her to return, she thought about what she would say and how much she would tell Clara. She wasn't even sure if Kim's accident really had to do with the typed story, or if it was just a coincidence. There was also the time she found the typewriter key in the garbage disposal. *What was that about?* All of it didn't make sense and she was determined to find out why all of this was happening.

As these questions circled around in her head, she saw Clara start to make her way back to where she was standing. Clara looked a little worried. Maybe her father said she wasn't allowed to leave his side. Maybe he saw Isobel standing there and did not want his daughter talking to her. Maybe *he* recognized her and wanted to keep hidden whatever secrets *he* had about the machine she had bought from them.

Clara tugged on Isobel's pant leg to snap her out of the trance she was in. "Ma'am," Clara got her attention as Isobel looked down. "Are you ready?"

Isobel looked down at her, "Yes, of course. Where do you want to go?"

"There is a store we can go to where no one will see or hear us," Clara said. "It's right around the corner."

Isobel knew exactly what store she meant. It had to be the Wawa she stopped at to ask for directions on her way into town judging by the direction Clara pointed when she mentioned it.

"Isn't that a little far?" she asked Clara. "We have to go on foot." She motioned her hand toward Clara's wheelchair.

"I can handle it ma'am," Clara said, "we need to be far away from here so no one can hear us talking."

Satisfied with that answer, Isobel agreed and the two of them made their way to the Wawa where Clara told Isobel about her horrifying experiences with the typewriter and her mother, Annie.

Clara was getting ready for school one Monday morning during her fifth-grade school year. She was dancing around her room to *Baby One More Time*, by Britney Spears. She was in a good mood because she loved her school. She had lots of friends and she usually got fairly decent grades. She was glad the weekend was over because Saturdays and Sundays were spent doing chores for her mother, who was very strict and did not let her go out to any friend's houses. Her mother Annie, kept Clara close at hand, but usually it was the back of her hand.

As Clara bounced and sashayed around in her room putting on her outfit for the day and gathering up her school books, she was singing along to the song, using a hairbrush as a microphone. She loved being silly behind her closed bedroom door where she thought her mom did not know what kind of shenanigans she was up to.

She needed to ask her mom for help with a button that fastened in the back of her shirt, so she went out of her room with her sneakers in her hand and walked two doors to the left in the hallway where Annie's room was, but she was not there. Clara went into her mother's bedroom to look around. She thought maybe her mom was getting dressed in her walk-in closet, but she was wrong. Annie was not in the closet either. In fact, she was nowhere to be found in her room.

Clara heard some shuffling around downstairs, so she knew her mother must already be down there waiting for her to come and have breakfast, which meant that Clara had to hurry up and get down there. Annie did *not* like to be kept waiting, especially when it was her daughter she was waiting for. She thought Clara fooled around too much in the mornings instead of getting ready for school like she was supposed to be doing.

Clara figured she better put her shoes on, grab her book bag, and go downstairs before her mom had to come looking for her because that never ended well. Still in her mom's bedroom, she sat down at the chair at Annie's desk so she could put on her sneakers. While she was bent over her legs reaching for the laces of her right shoe, the door to the bedroom slammed shut. There stood her mom, her face red with rage.

Clara looked up at her and began to cower in her seat because she knew what was about to happen. Annie's face was like a volcano ready to erupt as she started walking over to her daughter who was petrified.

"What did I tell you about messing with my typewriter?" Annie yelled at her.

"Mama," Clara said softly, "I didn't touch the ty..."

Annie interrupted her before she could plead her case. "YOU SHOULDN'T EVEN BE IN HERE!" she screamed as she back-handed Clara across the face.

Clara's nose started to instantly bleed and she began crying. "Please Mama. I swear, I didn't touch your typewriter."

Annie smacked her again, but this time it was on her back and Clara was knocked to the floor.

"Get up!" Annie pulled Clara's arm in order to stand her up, but then, pushed her backwards and Clara fell right into the Royal typewriter that was on the desk behind her. Her lower back slammed into its iron corner and she immediately collapsed to the floor.

"Mama," she cried, "I can't move. Please stop."

Annie tried to pick her up by her arm again, but Clara's legs just dangled under her. She could not get them to do what she wanted them to do, *stand*.

Annie put her back on the floor. Realizing her daughter was really hurt, she called an ambulance and threatened Clara not to say anything about how the injury really happened. She made up a story about Clara falling getting out of the shower as she frantically helped her continue to dress. Annie even went as far as getting a glass of water and wetting her daughter's hair with it so the shower story would be more believable.

Clara just continued to cry as she agreed to the absurd story of how it all happened. They lied to the ambulance crew and to everyone at the hospital as neither of them faltered from the story. It was obvious the doctor did not believe them, but Clara was terrified of her mother, so she said exactly what Annie wanted her to say. The doctor just ordered the appropriate tests so he could treat the child in front of him who was covered with bruises.

After a few agonizing hours at the hospital waiting for any news of Clara's test results, the doctor finally came in and asked if Clara's father was available to come in for a discussion. Annie quickly said no, as he was away at a convention selling some products from their small supply and electronic business.

Satisfied with that answer, the doctor just laid the news on Annie and Clara. Apparently, the fall caused some fractured vertebrae in Clara's lumbar spine. In Layman's terms, she had a broken back. The worst part of the news was that she would no longer be able to walk.

Clara's mind went into a fog as the news was being delivered. Clara was admitted to the hospital for three months, which were filled with drug therapies and lots of physical and mental therapy. When she was finally discharged, she left the hospital in a wheelchair she would never get up from.

Annie drove Clara home after the grueling hospital stay and, not a word was spoken between them the entire ten-minute drive as Clara tried to figure out how she would continue her life in a chair. *Will I play soccer anymore? Will I be able to play with my friends? Who will take care of me?* Her 11-year-old brain did not truly understand what her life would become, and her mom never even apologized, not even once.

When they returned home together, Annie helped Clara out of the car and into the wheelchair that would become her permanent means of mobility, now that she couldn't use her legs anymore to walk. She held her mother completely responsible for her handicap and would not speak to her at all.

The two of them managed to get into the house. It was a rough ride for Clara since her parents did not bother to put a ramp on the front of the house for her wheelchair. Annie had to pull her backwards up the three steps on the front of the house. Clara bounced so much with each step she almost fell out of her chair (her parents opted not to have the seatbelt option added to her wheelchair to try to keep the cost down).

When they finally got into the house Annie pushed Clara into the living room, turned the TV on, and left her in front of it without even asking her if she wanted to watch the TV. Clara didn't want to watch it. All she wanted to do was go up to her room and be alone, but she knew she couldn't get up there by herself and she was *not* going to ask her mother for help. She hated Annie for what she did to her, hated her with a *passion!*

After two hours and several sit-coms, Clara's father, Arthur, finally got home from work. He went right over to Clara and apologized for not being there when she was discharged from the hospital. Clara loved her dad and forgave him right away, but not before asking him to take her up to her bedroom. He picked her up out of her chair and set her on the couch.

"I'll take your chair up first," he said, "then I'll be back down for you. Okay, hun?"

"Yes, Daddy," she said.

Arthur took the wheelchair upstairs and came back for her, just like he said he would. She could always count on him. He gently picked her up and took her upstairs and put her back in her wheelchair by her bedroom window.

He looked at her and smiled. "Is this okay?" he asked.

"Yes," Clara looked at him and smiled, "I'll be fine here."

"Alright then I'm gonna go get cleaned up from work and I'll be back to check on you later." He winked at her and smiled as he backed out of her room.

Clara watched him leave her room and walk down the steps before she wheeled herself out of her room and into her parent's room. She had something she had to take care of and she could only do it in her mother's bedroom because that was where the only typewriter they owned was.

One of Clara's therapists at the hospital told her that a good way to get out a lot of your frustrations was to write about them to get them out of your system. She said that was the best thing to do if you couldn't express your anger out loud. Clara wanted to try out this theory, but she knew if she asked her mom for permission first, she would be told to stay away from Annie's things, *especially* her typewriter.

Clara wheeled herself into her parent's bedroom through their, already open bedroom door and went straight over to the Royal typewriter. She knew she didn't have a lot of time so she just started typing on the paper that was already loaded into the machine. She realized right away that the sound the keys made was pretty loud, so she stopped and went to the door and closed it so no one would hear what she was doing. The only reason she was in this situation in the first place was because Annie thought she had been messing with her stupid typewriter.

Clara quickly returned to the machine and began typing again. She typed about her accident and how it was entirely her stupid mother's fault, and how she hated her so much for everything. Her words flew onto the page like word vomit and before she knew it, her story had turned into a rant about how much she wished her mother would just die. She couldn't believe those words were coming out of her mind, but her therapist explained that some of the things she might write down will be things she didn't even realize she was thinking about in the first place. She explained how our truths can come out of our minds through our fingertips and onto the paper in front of us before we even are aware of what we are saying or thinking. Clara thought her doctor was off her rocker until it actually happened right in front of her.

Clara wrote about how much she hated her mother for the way she treated her and, *would it be too much to ask for her just to have an accident or something? Please, I want her out of my life.* Those words, among others filled up two full pages before Clara decided she had better get out of her parents' room before someone came up and caught her. She yanked the paper out of the typewriter and wheeled herself back into her own bedroom, where she folded the pages in half and placed them under her pillow.

Not long after Clara was back in her room comfortably looking out the window and wishing she was outside playing with the neighbor kids, who were kicking a ball around in a field that lined the back of the houses, she heard a blood curdling scream. It was her mother. Arthur flew up the steps, skipping two with each step, and went to Annie's aide.

After he calmed her down, they both went into their daughter's room to ask if she had been using the typewriter. Clara lied and said she had not been using it. That was when Annie showed Clara a paper she had pulled out of the typewriter. It had one single word typed on it.

A n n i e

Clara looked at the paper with confused eyes. She knew she was on that typewriter, but she did *not* type what she was looking at. She denied using the machine, even though she knew her mom didn't believe her. She wasn't sure if Arthur believed her or not, but he wasn't making a big deal about it, not like her mother was.

After he calmed Annie down, Arthur took her back into their bedroom where they talked for a while until he finally came out and asked Clara if she was hungry. Annie was too upset to make dinner so he offered to take Clara out to Burger King. She had not had a good greasy cheeseburger in a long time, so she jumped at her father's offer.

Annie sat on the edge of her bed, still raging at the thought of her ungrateful daughter messing with her typewriter. She did not know why Clara could not just leave things alone. If it had not been for Clara misbehaving, she would never have had to fight with her to the point her daughter's clumsiness made her fall and result in a major back injury.

She never took any responsibility when it came to the discipline of her daughter. Annie held Clara responsible for the outcomes of all of the beatings she had given her over the years.

Alone in her room, she was contemplating whether or not to go back downstairs or just stay in her room and get ready for bed. It was only seven in the evening, but she was exhausted from bringing her daughter home from the hospital and getting her into their house, which was not ready for a cripple. She looked at Clara as a cripple now and had absolutely no sympathy for her because she was getting all of the attention from everyone now. Annie was almost jealous of the daughter who she single-handedly put into this horrible situation.

She decided she didn't want to see her family anymore that evening so she reached down and slipped off her shoes. She was just going to get comfortable and stay upstairs. She slipped her feet into her slippers that were tucked halfway under her side of the bed.

With her slippers on, she ventured over to her dresser, which had a large mirror on top of it. It was one of those wide dressers that took up almost an entire wall. Annie kept her brushes, make-up and all of her little hair doohickeys on top of it so she could do her hair and make-up in her room instead of the bathroom. Her husband hated the clutter, but he left it alone to avoid arguments with his wife that he knew he could never win.

Annie opened the top center drawer where she kept her pajamas and took out a blue night gown. She looked at herself in the mirror and she could see the streaks on her face that were created by angry tears brought on by her ungrateful daughter. She grabbed her make-up remover from her make-up tray and leaned in close to the mirror to clean her face.

As she looked directly into the mirror she could see the Royal typewriter in the reflection behind her. The piece of paper with her name on it was lying next to it, face up so her name was prominently displayed. She could see it clearly and she quickly became enraged again. She stopped what she was doing and went over to the table where the machine was. She grabbed the paper with one hand, crinkled it up, and threw it into her trashcan before returning to the mirror to finish what she had started on her face.

She leaned in close to the mirror to see what she

was doing when she felt a chill as her body was surrounded by a sudden blast of cold air. It was as if someone had opened a window on a cold, blustery day. She pulled a sweater out of one of the bottom drawers of her dresser and quickly put it on. However, it did not help. Annie was freezing and could not figure out why.

Just as she was about to go check the thermostat on the bedroom wall, she felt someone, or something grab the back of her neck and she could not move. She knew no one was home and she knew she was not imagining it. It was as if there was a hand wrapped around the back of her neck and it was holding her so firmly she could not turn her head in either direction. She was forced to just stare directly at her own reflection in her mirror.

She struggled with no avail as her head just simply would not move, and before she knew it, the invisible force hastily pushed her forward and her face was launched into the center of the mirror sending shattered glass soaring in every direction.

Annie screamed as she struggled to remove her fleshy, bloody face from its landing place on the mirror. She was able to push off just enough to catch her gory reflection in a small shard of mirror that was still in place. Tears flooded her eyes and ran down the cuts on her cheeks, burning her face like the venom of a snake bite.

She was only able to get herself inches away from the smashed mirror before the unseen force returned and thrust her into the left-over fragments of the mirror before releasing her. She collapsed onto the floor like a ragdoll. Her bedroom floor had become a sheet of splintered glass, causing more lacerations to her back, legs, and arms.

As the blood drained from her body, her hazy eyes stared up at what was once her mirror and noticed one long single blade of glass hanging by a thread as it slowly moved back and forth before releasing itself from its platform. It found its way straight to Annie's chest as it landed on her, cutting deep into her flesh. Annie choked as blood came up out of her mouth. She laid on her bedroom floor in a pool of blood as her body became cold and her breaths became shallow. Annie succumbed to her injuries with no further struggle.

"That's how we found her," Clara said. "It was my typing that killed her."

Isobel's blank stare and gaping mouth were obvious signs of her surprise and disbelief at what Clara had told her for the last hour and a half.

"That's why my dad wanted to get rid of the typewriter," Clara said, "Are you alright, Lady?"

"Yes," Isobel said, "I just have one question."

Clara looked at her with questioning eyes, "What?"

"If your father wanted to get rid of it, why was it hiding in a box at the back of your business stand?"

Clara giggled, "My dad didn't want to have it out where people could play with it," she said. "He didn't want anyone typing on it because of what happened."

"But he let me buy it knowing it had problems?" Isobel looked at her watch and could not believe how much time had gone by. "We better get you back," she said "Your dad is probably worried sick."

The two of them headed back to the Green Acres fair, Isobel pushing Clara's wheelchair for the journey back. She wanted to hurry up and get the young girl back to her father so he didn't get worried, but; it was probably too late for that.

They did not talk any further and Isobel asked Clara if it was alright if she left her at the entranceway to the fair so she could get back to her car. Clara assured her that she would be okay because she knew her way back. She didn't seem concerned about the amount of time that had gone by. Isobel thought Clara's father must not be too strict with her. If Isobel had been out of her house for an unexplained amount of time Tom would not waste any time asking her where she had been, he would just beat the shit out of her.

She pushed Clara's wheelchair just inside the entrance to the fair and Clara took over from there.

"I got it," Clara said. "Bye."

"Goodbye," Isobel said "Thank you for the talk, Clara."

"No problem," Clara said as she pushed her wheels forward and left Isobel standing on the sidewalk.

Isobel quickly walked back down the street to where she had parked her car. She got in and started it up. She stared out the driver's side window and thought about all of the information she had just received.

She knew she could make the drive home in forty-five minutes, which would put her in her driveway just before lunchtime. Tom thought she was at work and he would not be home from work until about five, so she would have plenty of time to take care of a couple of things.

Isobel knew what she had to do and now she knew how to do it.

Isobel got home at twelve fifteen in the afternoon. She barely remembered her drive home because her mind was so preoccupied with Clara's story. It all made sense now. Arthur was so helpful with the purchase and delivery of the Royal because he was desperate to get rid of it. Isobel was not sure how she felt about that, but she was going to put her new knowledge to the test. She needed to know if it was just a one-time deal or if her typewriter had some kind of power she didn't understand.

She went upstairs to her bedroom and immediately took off her work clothes and put on some sweats. She sat down in front of the Royal and loaded a fresh sheet of paper into it and began to type. She knew what she wanted to type, but did not know exactly how to express what she wanted to say. Isobel's fingers just found their own way to the keys and started typing.

Before she knew it, Isobel had been typing for two hours. She had over six pages typed and all of them were about her husband's demise. Because of that little detail, she had to get rid of the evidence. She pulled the last sheet out of the Royal and ripped it up with the rest of the pages and threw them away in the bathroom trashcan. She knew Tom wouldn't look in there. God forbid he clean a bathroom, or *anything* for that matter, for once in his ungrateful life.

With the papers safely disposed of, Isobel went downstairs and turned on the TV. It was starting to cloud up outside as another storm was near. Comfortable on her sofa, she leaned back, put the news on the TV, and closed her eyes.

Before she could doze off, Isobel's eyes shot open and she was startled by the sound of thunder.

Tom left work right at five. He was tired from lack of sleep the previous night due to the storm and the fight with his wife. He got in his truck and drove out of the parking area of his job site. He honked his horn at the few guys, who had gathered by their cars to chat. He partially opened his window and stuck his hand out to wave as he pulled out onto the highway.

He inserted an AC/DC compact disk into his CD player and with *Highway to Hell* blaring out of his speakers, he stepped on the gas to propel himself past a couple of cars that were not driving up to his standards. Tom never obeyed the speed limits and he never got pulled over by the police, so he thought he was invincible. He only wore his seatbelt sometimes and this was one of the occasions he opted not to wear it.

Tom only had a short drive home, but he saw some dark clouds ahead. He hated thunderstorms, and it looked like they were about to get another doozy. As he looked out ahead, he saw some lightning zigzag through the sky. It seemed to be off in the distance and he thought he would probably be home before it hit.

He could not have been more wrong. The storm rolled in quicker than he had ever seen, and before he knew it, buckets of rain drops were pouring down his windshield faster than his windshield wipers were able to brush them away. The rain was coming down so hard and loud he could not hear his music, so he turned it off so he could concentrate on driving.

Every second the rain seemed to be getting worse. Tom was driving further into the middle of the worst thunder storm he had ever driven in. His ride was becoming bumpy as his tires sloshed through the large puddles that were forming on the road. His truck had slowed down to a crawl and he could not see anything out in front of him, except for the bright flashes of lightning that were lighting up the sky like a strobe light.

After driving in the ruckus for five minutes (which felt like an hour), Tom looked over to the side of the road to see if he could find a place to pull off and let the storm pass, but he could barely see anything as the water continued to smack his truck's windows from all directions. As he looked to the side he heard something in the back seat of his truck that sounded like something had fallen onto the floor. He turned his head around for a brief moment, but saw nothing on the floor behind him.

When Tom regained his focus on the blurry watered-down highway, he felt something poking his thigh from underneath him. It felt like something was in his seat cushion so he moved his leg aside to check it out. As soon as he shifted in his seat, there was another disturbance in the truck. Tom felt a light scratching sensation on his neck that startled him, and he jumped and whatever it was, fell behind him in the seat. He could hear it rustling around behind him.

His Ford pickup was swerving between two lanes on the highway as Tom struggled to see what was with him in his seat. He could not pull the truck to the side of the road because the visibility was so poor. Instead of trying to look behind himself, he shoved his hand behind his back, but his reach was cut short by a sharp, piercing pain that suddenly struck his middle finger, causing Tom to yank his hand back out. Something bit him and blood was dripping from his finger onto his jeans.

Whatever it was, he didn't feel it behind him anymore so he punched the glove compartment to jolt it open. He knew he had paper towels in there. Whenever he went to a fast-food joint he hoarded their napkins, so he had a pretty decent supply.

As soon as the door to the glove compartment opened, it became obvious what had bitten him because there were two more of them in there. They stared at him with their red, beady eyes. Rats! Tom's biggest fear looked up at him as if they were plotting their next move, but the two in the glove compartment soon became the least of his worries when he looked down at his body and realized the rest of their beastly family was crawling all over him. He could actually hear their high-pitched squeaks over the rain that was pelting his truck from every direction.

Tom frantically started pushing the rodents off his legs and kicking them away from his feet. One had become lodged under the brake pedal making it difficult for Tom to step on it and slow down. He was losing control of the situation. The truck had sped up and was now cruising at just over eighty miles per hour.

Tom reached for his door handle to try to push some of the rats out onto the road, but he was only able to grasp the body of another rat that had planted itself in the pocket of the door. Tom panicked as he looked all around the cab of his truck and saw nothing but rats, and they all seemed to want a piece of him. He swatted at them, kicked at them, and screamed at them, but nothing worked. It only made them angrier.

"WHERE THE FUCK DID YOU COME FROM?" He screamed as his battle continued. "GET THE FUCK OFF ME FUCKERS!"

His truck was so infested with rats at that point and he could no longer even see his windshield as they piled up on the dashboard in front of him. Tom's heart raced and he was pouring with sweat as he continued to drive, flailing his arms and yelling, while at the same time wondering what was with these rats in his life lately as this was his second run-in with them in less than a week.

The fat-bodied rat that had been sitting under the brake pedal finally dislodged itself, but just when Tom found the pedal with his boot, another rat jumped onto his face and started gnawing on his chin causing Tom to completely lose control of his truck. He drifted off the side of the road, and slammed into a parked tractor trailer at full speed. Tom was killed instantly as his airbag deployed and slammed his head back into his seat.

There was a man sitting in the tractor trailer who got out and called 911 when he saw and felt the wreck that was embedded into the back of his truck. All that was left of the storm were a few remnants of puddles that were left behind on the road's shoulder.

As the trucker approached the pickup truck he saw someone in the driver's seat that was leaning against the driver's side window with the deflated airbag in front of him. He didn't hear any emergency vehicles yet, and he knew whoever was in the truck needed to get out because he smelled gas.

Putting his own safety aside, the trucker went over to the door where he had a clear view of the driver. He nervously reached for the door handle so he could help the person. When his hand found the handle he quickly pulled on it, but the door was stuck.

The trucker could clearly see that the man inside the Ford pickup was not moving. He could not see his face though, all he could see was the top of his head and his body, which appeared to be trapped by the steering wheel, which was crammed down into the guy's lap.

He made a second attempt to open the door. With all his strength, he yanked on the handle again, and this time it opened just enough for him to see that the driver was not conscious. The trucker gave it one final pull. The door finally opened just far enough for the truck driver to see what he was actually dealing with.

Tom's lifeless body fell limply to the side as his head hit the door, while his legs remained trapped inside the vehicle between the steering wheel and the driver's seat. Other than an obvious broken nose which was probably caused by the air bag, there was not another mark on Tom's body. The trucker stepped back, knowing he could not help the man at that point. He got his phone out of his pocket again to check on the ambulance, but he did not dial, as he could hear the sirens of emergency vehicles approaching the scene.

Isobel was jolted awake to see an advertisement for Downy laundry soap on the TV. The commercial was so loud, it made her jump. It always seemed like the commercials were so much louder than whatever show was on. They do this as a way to get the attention of the viewers, but in most cases, it just pisses people off, at least that's how Isobel felt.

She must have dozed off; she had no idea what time it was. She got up from the sofa and looked at the clock on the wall. It was seven. Tom should have been home a while ago, but she wasn't too worried about it because he had a habit of wandering off. He didn't even care enough to let her know where he was.

Isobel looked outside to see if his truck was in the driveway, thinking he could be next door with Kim. When she did not see his truck, and noticed how dark the neighbor's house was, she remembered Kim was not home. She was in the hospital and that was probably where her dumb-ass husband was as well since, he had a crush on that woman.

Isobel went to the steps to climb the stairs, but a sudden knock on her front door halted her. She looked through the peephole on the door and saw two police officers standing on her front porch. She hesitantly reached for the doorknob and slowly opened the door.

When the officers saw her, they immediately removed their hats from their heads as Isobel pushed open the storm door.

"Can I help you?" She asked.

One of the officers looked at her but it seemed he did not want to look directly into her eyes. "Are you Mrs. Parrish?" He asked as his eyes slowly raised up to meet hers.

Isobel said, "Yes," as she looked over the man's shoulder to brace herself for the next thing that would come out of his mouth. She knew what he was going to say before he said it.

The officer did not waste any time before he just blurted it out. "I'm sorry to have to tell you this, but your husband was in an accident."

The second officer stayed silent as his partner delivered the supposedly devastating news to the newly widowed woman in front of them.

Isobel appeared to be fighting back her tears and she did not say a word. She just bowed her head down and looked at the ground. She listened as the officer said he was sorry again, but all she could think about was the mud that was caked on the police officer's shoe. He looked clean and pressed, except for his right shoe. There was no reason to be fixated on the shoe, other than to avoid looking at him.

Not knowing what to say, she thanked the gentlemen and slowly closed the front door, still not a tear in her eyes. She stood in the foyer for a moment and watched them drive away before turning to go upstairs like she was planning before she was interrupted.

When she got to her bedroom, she avoided going over to her typewriter. She didn't know if she was scared of the machine at that point, or if she just did not want to see, or admit, the fact she may have caused Tom's accident.

Isobel got into the shower (something she hadn't been able to do at her leisure for a long time), and as the hot water ran over her head, the tears finally came. However, they were not tears of sadness. Isobel Parrish found herself audibly laughing in the shower as she washed away the remnants of the day and the last of the bruises she would ever receive at the hands of Tom Parrish.

She showered for twenty minutes, the longest she had been able to shower since before she was married. She got out and wrapped herself in a towel while wrapping another towel around her head to dry her hair before she went back into her bedroom to put on one of her nightgowns that she hadn't been able to wear for a long time. Tom always made her wear raggedy things, even to bed.

In her sexy nightgown with her hair just dry enough so it wouldn't drip on her nighty, she moved to stand in front of the Royal. She jumped when she saw what was typed on the single sheet of paper that was loaded into the machine. She was surprised at how *not* surprised she actually was to see it. She was not sure exactly *how* she was supposed to feel when she saw the word:

T O M

typed in capital letters in the middle of the page. She was not scared and she was not sad. In fact, she felt more relaxed than she had in years.

Isobel got into bed and comfortably covered herself up with her blankets as she fluffed her pillow to cradle her head. She got the best night's sleep she had gotten in years that night.

Carissa and Carol were standing at the coffee pot getting their morning coffee and chatting when the bell jingled at the door of Humphrey's Homes, signaling someone's arrival. Both of them looked over to see who it was, and they were shocked to see the woman who walked in the door to their office.

She was dressed in a red business casual dress with a white halter sweater over the top half. Her shoes were as red as her dress and her slender legs, covered only by nylons, were visible up to the knees. The woman had her blonde hair pulled back into a bun that made it possible to show off her silver hoop earrings. Her makeup was only subtly applied. It was just enough to give her an extra appeal that she probably did not need because the woman was stunning.

As they stared in awe at the beauty in the doorway of Humphrey's Homes, they both dropped their jaws when they realized it was Isobel.

She walked right over to her desk and put her purse, which was the exact shade of red as her outfit, on her desk before going over to the coffee pot to get her morning dose of caffeine. She didn't say a word to anyone as she poured her much-needed cup of coffee like it was just another day at the office.

Carol spoke up first. "You look good Isobel," she

said as she slightly shrugged her shoulders and looked at Carissa.

"Thank you," she said as she turned to go back to her desk "Just trying to wear some of my things that have been tucked away in the closet."

"Well it looks great," Carissa chimed in. "And I love your hair that way. You should wear it like that more often."

Isobel looked at both of them and smiled. "I think I will. As a matter of fact, I think I will be making a lot of changes." She walked away from the coffee station leaving both of the ladies stunned.

When Mr. Humphrey arrived a short time later, it was more of the same. He complimented Isobel on the way she looked, and even made a statement about how happy she seemed. He knew she was normally shy and unhappy due to her home life with a husband who obviously beat her. He had also noticed her constant bruises, but like everyone else, he tried to mind his own business.

Isobel did her job that day with a smile on her face that no one could take away. Even the nasty customers she had to deal with on the phone from time to time could not upset her. She answered and transferred calls, as was her job, and set up a few appointments for people to come in and talk to the agents about buying a new home. She had not been that happy for a long time. She knew everyone had noticed, not only her attire, but how happy she was also.

The morning at work flew by as Isobel was inundated with phone calls, and she had two reports to type for her boss. She didn't even realize when lunchtime arrived. Carissa came over to her desk and asked if she wanted to grab a bite to eat with her. Isobel immediately logged off her computer and accepted the invitation. They went to a nearby Burger King, which was not Isobel's first choice (she hated fast food joints), but she was thrilled to not be having lunch alone and she was not in a position to turn away any friends since she didn't have any. Once they received their food and sat down at one of the window tables, Carissa looked at Isobel and seized her moment. She had to find out about the sudden change in her coworker's demeanor.

"So," she started, "How are you today? You look great and you seem happy," Carissa said as she looked at her with questioning eyes.

"I'm good," Isobel said, "I just thought I would dress up a little today. I'm tired of looking like a ragdoll all the time."

Carissa took a large gulp of the Diet Pepsi she ordered with her cheeseburger. When she returned her cup to the table she started probing, "Yeah, but I thought you would probably be tired today, and that maybe you would call out of work."

"Now, why would I do that?" Isobel asked.

"Mr. Humphrey said you went home yesterday to take care of your husband." Carissa put a French fry in her mouth and spoke between chews, "Wasn't he sick or something?"

Isobel started eating her cheeseburger in an attempt to avoid answering the question. She looked at Carissa and finally said, "Yes, I did, but he is better now."

"I don't know why you would want to take care of him anyway," Carissa said, taking the chance of making her coworker mad, "with the way he treats you all the time."

"What are you talking about?" Isobel asked, offended.

"C'mon Isobel, we see the bruises you try to cover up all the time."

"I don't know what you..."

Carissa did not let her finish speaking before she continued. "And you're sad all the time."

Isobel continued eating and she turned to look out the window to avoid making eye contact with her coworker. She didn't know how to handle these questions, not with what happened yesterday. Should she tell Carissa what happened? It was only a matter of time before everyone found out that Tom was dead. But she couldn't tell her now. How would she explain her happiness if Carissa knew that her husband had just died? Not knowing how to handle the third degree she was getting, she picked up her soda and said, "We should get back."

Carissa looked puzzled because they still had plenty of time before they needed to return to work. They had a full hour for lunch and the Burger King was only a five-minute drive from the office. They had only been there for fifteen minutes or so. She looked at her watch and said, "We have some time."

"Yeah, but I have to get back and make a phone call before I start back to work this afternoon," she lied.

They packed up their garbage from their half-eaten lunches and threw it in the trashcan by the entrance door to the restaurant. They took their sodas with them out the door and headed to Carissa's car, neither one of them saying another word. They simply got into Carissa's car and drove back to the office, both of them still hungry.

When they returned, Carol was standing on the front sidewalk of the building talking on her cellphone. She was giggling in a giddy way that was usually reserved for high school girls when they flirted with the cute boys. Carissa and Isobel walked past her and went in the front door of Humphrey's Homes where the dangling bell announced their arrival. It was a little annoying, but the ladies were used to it. It didn't faze them anymore, but it did get Mr. Humphrey's attention, which was quickly returned back to his phone call when he realized it was just his employees coming back from lunch.

Carol came in the front door shortly after the women got back to their seats. Isobel was on the phone so she went over to talk to Carissa.

"How was lunch?" she asked.

"It was fine," Carissa said, "We just went to Burger King."

"You guys are back early."

Carissa looked over at Isobel to see if she was still

on the phone. She didn't want her to hear what she was about to say. "Yeah, Isobel said she had to get back to make a phone call," she whispered.

"What's the matter?" Carol asked. She could tell by the way her friend was speaking quietly that she was trying not to be heard.

Carissa looked at her and whispered, "Do you think Isobel is acting strange today?" she asked.

"Yeah, a little. Maybe she just wanted to look nice today."

"I'm not talking about the way she looks," Carissa hastily said. "Have you noticed how happy she is today?"

"I haven't paid that much attention, but she did seem different this morning when we were getting coffee."

Isobel ended her fake phone call and walked toward the chatty women. She was headed to the restroom, which was just past Carissa's desk. Her approach put the ladies' conversation to an instant halt.

When Isobel came out of the restroom she walked right past the women, who were no longer talking, and returned to her desk. Carissa and Carol delved back into their work and their conversation never resumed for the rest of the day. Carol actually left work an hour early that day because she had a date that everyone in the office knew about. She was excited about this new guy she had been seeing, but no one knew who he was. She was so secretive about that part. She left at four because she had a forty-five-minute drive to get home and he was meeting her there.

With Carol gone for the day, the office was quiet. There was no chit chat amongst Carissa and Isobel and the phones had been silent. There were only two phone calls in that last hour of the work day and both were only inquiring about the hours of operation for the real estate company. When five o'clock finally arrived (Isobel worked until five on Tuesdays), Isobel was already logged off her computer. She logged off a few minutes early so she could leave right away without being asked any more questions. She had to go home and think about how she was going to handle telling people that Tom was dead, and how she would handle her attitude. Obviously, she had to adjust her mood into a more somber one, at least temporarily.

When Isobel got home, the house phone was ringing. She could hear it from the driveway as soon as she got out of her car. She quickly closed her car door without locking it and ran to the front door where she had to fumble with her keys to find the right one. Of course, she dropped them right when she found it.

"Shit!" she said as she squatted down on her front porch to pick them up. She got lucky and found the front door key in her hands right away when she stood up. Isobel opened the door and entered the house just in time to hear the last ring before the answering machine would have answered it. She picked up the phone.

"Hello?" she said, out of breath, but there was no one on the other end. She had just missed the call and they did not have caller ID. Tom thought it was a waste of money.

Isobel dropped her purse on the kitchen counter and trudged up the stairs to her bedroom so she could change out of her work clothes. She had to start planning a funeral. She also had to come up with a good reason for being at work the day after her husband died, instead of staying home to mourn. Not only did she go to work, but she was happy that day.

In her room, the phone next to her bed started ringing. She quickly answered it. "Hello?"

"Mrs. Parrish?" a male voice asked from the other end of the line.

"Yes?" she asked, curious about who would be calling her.

"My name is Sergeant Macintyre, I am calling, first to tell you how sorry we are for your loss."

Isobel wondered how sorry he could actually be. He didn't even know her, but she replied, "Thank you."

Sergeant Macintyre sounded so official, but she knew it was his job. "I must inform you that your husband's body has been taken to the Maryland state coroner's office for an autopsy."

"Why?" Isobel asked.

"The way he was found does not indicate an obvious cause of death," he said.

"What do you mean? He was in an accident in his truck."

"Yes, but the way the crash occurred raises suspicion of drugs or alcohol," he explained. "He also could have fallen asleep at the wheel, or there may have been an underlying health condition that could have rendered him unconscious before the accident. It is our job to find out the exact cause of death in these cases."

Isobel didn't really know what to say to all of that, so she asked what she thought anyone in her situation might ask. "What about his funeral?"

"You can make the arrangements as you need to," Sergeant Macintyre assured her. "His body will be released after the autopsy, which usually takes about a week. Then we will take him to the funeral home of your choosing."

"Okay," Isobel said "Thank you for calling. Is there anything I need to do?"

"No. We'll call you when he has arrived at the funeral home. Just call our office and tell the receptionist where you want him sent. We will do the rest."

Isobel thanked him and he offered his condolences once more before ending the call. For a moment, she thought he was going to ask her to come identify Tom's body. *Isn't that what they usually do? Maybe that was just in the movies.* Isobel stood frozen by the phone for a few minutes while these thoughts raced through her mind. She also thought it might be a good idea, while she was still near the phone, to call her boss and tell him of Tom's death, so she could stay home from work for a couple of days to mourn. She knew she had to do that, especially after the way she acted at work that day.

Isobel worked up some fake tears, which, to her surprise, became real tears as she dialed Mr. Humphrey's phone number. The phone rang three times before he picked up.

"Hello?"

"Mr. Humphrey?" Isobel's sniffles made it hard for her boss to identify her voice.

"Yes," he said.

"It's Isobel." She was crying full-force by this time. "I won't make it in tomorrow."

"Is everything alright, Isobel?"

"No," she sniffed and blew her nose. "Tom was killed in an accident." She offered no more information as to when, where, or how.

Mr. Humphrey, not wanting to pry or upset her any further said, "Oh my God! I'm so sorry," he paused before continuing, "Please let me know if there is anything I can do for you, and please take all the time you need."

"Thank you," Isobel said and she abruptly hung up the phone.

She stood frozen, looking at the phone for a moment before walking to her closet to get changed. On her way across the floor, she stopped in front of the typewriter where her husband's name was still printed on the paper. A sudden chill ran through her entire body as she pulled the paper out of the machine, crinkled it up, and threw it in the trashcan.

She went into the bathroom to get a tissue because she couldn't seem to stop crying. She was glad Tom was gone, but he was still her husband and there was a time when she loved him more than anything in the world. He *was* her world and she searched her mind for the moment that changed. She could not remember exactly when, or what happened, but for years she has had to endure his abuse and *that* is what she needed to focus on now to justify his untimely death that she knew she had caused. *Or had the Royal caused it?*

When she went back into her room, she noticed a definite temperature drop. It was so cold in there.

She didn't remember it being like that when she first went upstairs. She wrapped her robe around herself after putting on some jeans and a sweatshirt, although it didn't seem to help. She cupped her hands in front of her mouth as she blew warm air into them to warm them up.

This is ridiculous. She thought as she checked the thermostat again and saw that it read sixty-nine degrees, which was the same temperature she always had it set on. *What the hell? It's not even cold outside.* Isobel left her room and went downstairs where she knew it was warmer.

After making herself a sandwich for dinner (she didn't have to cook anything now that Tom was gone), Isobel turned on the TV just in time for *Family Feud*. She loved Steve Harvey and she desperately needed some cheering up. He never disappointed with his opening line, "We've got a great one for you today." He always said that right before introducing the families that would be playing that night.

She sat on her sofa and ate her sandwich and some chips while answering the questions that were asked of the families during the show. After watching three episodes back to back (the Game Show Network always played several episodes of Family Feud in a row), Isobel decided she was tired and made her way upstairs to bed with heavy thoughts of how she would handle herself over the next few days.

As she took her robe off and reached for a pair of

sweatpants that were on her bed, something caught her eye on the table where the Royal sat. There was a blank sheet of white paper loaded into it that she did not remember putting there. As a matter of fact, she *knew* she hadn't put it there, but she left it alone and crawled into bed so she could bundle up under her covers and try to sleep in her frigid bedroom.

Isobel awoke suddenly in the middle of the night to a sound like a twig snapping in half. She sat up in bed and turned on the lamp on her nightstand. She looked around her room and could not figure out where the noise had come from, so she got out of bed and made her way slowly to the bedroom door, where she peeked her head halfway out to see if she could see or hear anything. When she was sure there was nothing there, she walked back over to her bed, but right before she reached the bed, a sudden jolt of pain rushed through her foot as she stepped on something.

She leaned on her bed while picking up her right foot to see what it was. It felt like it was still there and she was right. She reached down and pulled the black object from the bottom of her foot and brought it up to the light so she could see what it was. As she held it close, she could clearly see that it was one of the keys from her typewriter. The C key was on her floor, but before she could theorize how it could have possibly gotten there, she had to take care of her foot which was bleeding. She caught a drop of blood with a tissue she had gotten out of the bathroom before it dripped onto the floor.

Isobel limped back into the bathroom where she put her foot into the bathtub and rinsed it off with cold water. She had put the typewriter key on the table with the typewriter before she went in there. As she watched the water in the tub run over her foot and turn from red to a light pink, her mind was overcome with thoughts as to how the key fell on the floor. Too tired to stress over it, she dried her foot off and went back to bed, but not before covering up the Royal with a dry towel from the bathroom. The machine was starting to creep her out.

Isobel thought of Clara's story of her experience with the typewriter and her mother's death, and how she thought the Royal had crippled her. It sounded crazy at the time, but now, strange things were happening right in front of Isobel.

With her mind uneasy, she climbed into bed, covered up with her comforter in her cold room, and drifted off to sleep. The Royal, which was now covered, sat on the table next to her with the 'C' from its own keyboard sitting next to it like it was watching Isobel. She didn't sleep much that night.

The next day, Isobel did not have to go to work, as she had spoken with her boss already, but she knew he would not arrive at the office until after everyone else was already there. She thought it would be a good idea to call the office and let the staff know she would not be coming in so they wouldn't worry. Isobel was *never* late.

She called the office in the morning and Carol answered the phone, which was surprising because she was usually the last one in. "Good morning. Humphrey's Homes," she said.

"Hi Carol," Isobel said, "I'm not going to make it in today. I had a family emergency. I already spoke with Mr. Humphrey about it."

"Okay," Carol said, "Is there anything I can do?"

"No," Isobel said, "I'll be fine. I don't know if I will be in tomorrow either. Can you and Carissa handle the incoming phone calls for a couple of days?"

"Sure. Please let us know if there is anything we can do," Carol was sweet, even though Isobel knew she didn't like her very much.

"Thanks," Isobel said as she abruptly hung up the phone.

She stood there alone in her kitchen looking at the phone and listening to the quiet of the house. *Is this real?* She felt she should be able to hear the sound of

Tom hollering at her or kicking something to get it out of his way. It had not yet completely sunk in that her husband, the man who abused her for several years, was really gone. *Am I really alone with no one telling me what to do?* These thoughts circled her mind as she stood still and listened for something, anything to indicate it had all been a dream.

Isobel looked out the window above her kitchen sink, the same window she would see Tom flirting with the neighbor through. Oh, Kim, that was another story. Isobel leaned in closer to the window, sure she would see or hear someone outside, but not even Kim's dog was barking. Nothing... she heard absolutely nothing.

The stillness of the house was both creepy and comforting at the same time. Isobel turned away from the window and looked into the empty kitchen, still listening. Everything was peaceful and she didn't want the moment to end, so she closed her eyes and took a deep breath.

Suddenly, a deafening, thunderous boom erupted and shook the entire house. Isobel's heart skipped a beat as she jumped and steadied herself on the counter.

It took a few seconds for her to collect her composure before she realized that, whatever the hellacious sound was, it came from upstairs. She slowly walked toward the foot of the steps, not sure if she was going to go up them or not. Her internal debate continued as she inched closer and closer to the place where she would have to make a decision. *To go up, or not go up?*

The thought made her briefly smile as she thought of Shakespeare and Hamlet's soliloquy. Then, reality slapped her with an open hand.

Isobel stood still and listened, but there was no more noise. In fact, she had not heard *anything* since the sonic boom that shook her house like an earthquake with a magnitude of 3.0, so she thought it would be safe to venture upstairs. She slowly crept up the steps as if she were sneaking up on an intruder, which was another thought she had in the back of her mind. *What if someone is up there?*

As she approached the top of the landing, she noticed another definite temperature drop (which was getting to be a normal thing). She wrapped her arms around herself as the chill in the air enveloped her body. Isobel was shivering full force by the time she placed her feet on the carpet of the second floor. She looked around to see if she could see anything that could have made that atrocious noise, but her eyes came up empty. All she saw was carpet and the open doorways to the bathroom and the two bedrooms that were up there, hers being one of them.

When she realized that her view from the stairs allowed her to see into the bathroom and the guest bedroom, where she did not see anything out of place, she knew she would have to go into *her* room, the room she could not see into. Without any further hesitation, she walked straight into her bedroom.

It didn't take long to figure out what had happened.

Isobel gasped like she had just seen a ghost, at the catastrophe that was strewn all over the floor. The Royal typewriter, *her* Royal typewriter, lay on the floor as if someone picked it up and threw it down with all their might. Its body was upside down, the keys were scattered from wall to wall, the interior mechanisms (which Isobel did not know the names of yet) were disassembled and spread around the frame, and even the paper that was on the table was scattered all over the place as if a gust of wind blew in the window, but the window was shut.

Isobel stared at the horrific sight in disbelief as she continued to try to warm herself up in the cool air that was now becoming commonplace in her bedroom. It took a couple of minutes before she gingerly tip-toed through the wreckage to get to her chair in front of the table where the typewriter sat earlier that day. She sat in the chair and reached down to pick up the Royal's body to put it back on the table. Although it was not as heavy now that all of its parts were on the floor, it still had *some* weight to it, but that did not stop Isobel from being able to put it where she wanted it.

She set the machine down and it scratched the surface of her nice writing table with its bent frame. Not sure what to do with the rest of the debris that surrounded her as the Royal lay in disarray on the floor, Isobel propped her elbow up on the table and rested her chin in the palm of her hand as she studied the remains of what, she was sure, was responsible for Tom's

141

death (with a little help from her, maybe). There was no way she was going to be able to put the thing back together, and the more she thought about it, the more she thought that maybe she *shouldn't* put it back together anyway. *Didn't I get what I wanted out of it? What good would it do to keep it around?* As she pondered over these questions, the idea of the Royal having some kind of power that *she* controlled was beginning to sound not only crazy, but also intriguing.

She sat in her room for a while as her mind wandered in different directions. She had lots to think about, but first of all, she had to plan a funeral for her husband. She decided she would go downstairs (where it was warm) and make a few phone calls to get the ball rolling on that, but just when she turned in her chair to stand up, she heard a small noise like the flutter of a beetle's wings. It startled her and it only lasted a few seconds. Then, there was silence again.

As she looked around the room to try to figure out what the sound was, she heard it again; only this time, she could tell it was coming from the center of the pile of pieces on the floor, but she could not pin-point exactly where. She thought there was something stuck under one of the typewriter's pieces.

Isobel stood up and made her way over to the area she thought the sound was coming from, and she saw a few of the mangled typewriter keys shaking and sliding against each other as if they were blades of grass blowing in a light breeze. There was no reasonable explanation for them to be moving the way they were so she reached down to pick them up, but stopped suddenly when the keys elevated off the floor all by themselves.

Isobel stood frozen in terror as the keys slowly circled around her. She watched in disbelief and was afraid to move from the place she stood. She trembled from head to toe as she studied what was happening right in front of her. The keys suddenly shifted from the counterclockwise motion they were making around Isobel's frozen body, and suddenly darted right in front of her face, landing inside the center of the bruised body of the Royal on the table. It all happened so fast she had no time to react, or try to theorize what the hell was happening.

A swift chill overtook Isobel's body as she stepped back over to the table. She turned around slowly with her eyes wide open in a hypnotic state and looked blankly at the floor. One by one the fragments of the machine lifted off the floor and flew toward her where she stood. None of them hit her. Their destination was the table. Isobel did not turn around or duck as all of the machine's parts continued to come at her like a swarm of flies.

The entire episode took only three or four minutes before the mess was off the floor completely and surrounding the Royal on the table behind her. She slowly turned around and directed her eyes to the table, taking a step backward as she continued to stare at the Royal.

Still astounded, her eyes did not move from the Royal as its body started to straighten out its corners one by one until the body was neatly together and undamaged sitting on the table. That was when the unreal and unimaginable happened, as if things could get stranger. Isobel did not move a muscle as the rest of the pieces lifted off the table and placed themselves back into position in the typewriter until the entire thing was put back together as if nothing had ever happened.

She blinked her eyes as her stupor state left her body. When she was lucid again, she held her hand to her mouth as if holding herself back from screaming. She had no recollection of what she had just seen. The last thing she remembered was the Royal in shambles all over the floor.

Isobel was frightened and she quickly went into her bathroom to retrieve the towel she had used to cover the thing up. She threw the towel over the machine and quickly left her room, and ran downstairs so fast she was out of breath. When she reached the kitchen, she poured herself a glass of water. She sipped the water as she tried to make sense out of the events that just happened. She knew she did not put the Royal back together and she struggled for any explanation of how it happened. *Could someone else have come in and fixed it?* Her mind was racing as her heart thundered in her chest.

She stood by the sink drinking the last of her water when there was an unexpected pounding on her front door. Isobel jumped and the glass of water slipped out of her hand and went crashing to the floor sending shards of glass all around the place she was standing. She carefully stepped over the glass and peeked out the window to see if she could see who could possibly be at her door. She could not tell who it was, so she walked over to the front door and hesitantly reached for the door knob as if she was about to put her hand into a snake pit.

Isobel grasped the door knob, still shaking with fear, and slowly turned it, barely making a sound. She cracked the door open just enough to see the man who was standing on her porch.

John stood at the door with his dog Bentley. He had the look of a child who had just dropped his ice cream cone on the ground when he looked at Isobel. It was obvious he did not know what to say and Isobel could not, for the life of her, figure out why he would be at her door.

She knew she would have to break the awkward silence between them. "Can I help you?" she asked him as he continued to stand speechless at her door. "Are you alright?"

"Is Tom here?" he finally asked.

Isobel was not sure how to address the subject of her husband's death. "I'm sorry," she said as she looked down at her feet, "I guess you haven't heard."

"Heard what?"

Not knowing exactly what to say, she just blurted it out. "Tom was killed in an accident. I guess you haven't watched the news?" she asked.

He looked as if he was searching for words. "Oh," he said, "I'm so sorry."

"Thank you," Isobel said as she lifted her eyes from the floor to meet his. "How is Kim?" she asked in an attempt to change the subject.

"I just brought her home from the hospital and I need someone to help me get her upstairs to bed," he said, "I just need someone to spot me or walk behind us as we go upstairs. I have a bad back."

This was the first she had heard of his bad back. But, how could she have known? She barely knew her neighbors. "I'm so sorry about what happened to her," Isobel said, even though she *was* kind of responsible for Kim's intentional accident, but it didn't matter anymore. Tom was dead.

"Thank you," he said, "She is in bad shape and pretty drugged up at the moment."

Isobel felt bad for him. "Would you like me to come over and help you?"

"You don't mind?" he asked, "After what you've been through? I don't want to be a bother to you."

Bentley decided to lie down at their feet as the conversation became boring and too long for him. He was a well-behaved dog.

"Really, it's alright" she insisted, "I have to get out of this house for a little while anyway."

He agreed and she stepped out onto the porch and closed the door behind her. They walked in reticence to John and Kim's house as neither of them knew what else to say. They were both facing their own demons: John, with his guilty feelings about not spending enough time with his wife, and Isobel, with her knowledge of how both of their spouse's accidents occurred, and even having a hand in it.

They walked in the front door of John's home and Isobel was surprised to see Kim sitting upright on the sofa. Their living room sofa was in plain view as soon as they entered the front door.

Kim was sitting up with her hands folded in her lap. The sun shone through a nearby window casting a halo around her head that made her blonde hair so bright and beautiful that Isobel did not notice the bandages that still covered her face, not at first anyway; then, they walked toward her. Kim just stared forward as if she didn't see anyone coming. Isobel wondered if the burns had affected her eye sight.

She paused as John continued toward his wife. Kim appeared to see him as he got closer to her.

"I brought someone over to help," he said to Kim, "I want to get you upstairs so you can rest."

"No! I don't want anyone to see me like this!"

John took her hand in his and calmly said, "the doctor said you have to rest."

He couldn't get another word out before she interrupted him, "I don't want to go to bed."

"But the doctor..."

"I've been in bed for days!" she hollered at him. "Who is here?"

"It's Isobel from next door."

Isobel took the opportunity to walk into the living room. "I'm right here," she said.

Kim looked at her, eyes straining to see. "I'm sorry Isobel, but I don't need your help. I'm sorry my husband bothered you."

"Are you sure?" Isobel asked. "I don't mind, and

there is something I want to talk to you about, if you're up to it."

Kim did not say anything for a few moments. Her reluctance to answer gave Isobel time to see some of the damage to the uncovered part of the woman's face. There was still a bandage that ran over her chin, covering her entire neck, as well as one on her left cheek that also covered her nose. The only opening was where her nostrils were, obviously so she could breathe. The bare skin in that area was visible just enough for Isobel to see the rawness, as well as a blister that was just below Kim's left nostril that was so red and filled with puss it looked like it would explode at any moment.

Kim finally looked at Isobel as she asked, "What could you possibly have to talk to me about?"

Isobel chickened out of telling her that Tom was dead and that she would have to find someone else's husband to flirt with, "How are you feeling," even though she already knew the answer to that question.

I've just had my fucking face burnt off! How the fuck do you think I feel?

"I'm getting a little better. I don't really have much feeling in my face right now, but that will come back." She looked at her husband. "Can you help me up?"

John went to her, took her hands, and helped her to her feet. He gently kissed her on the forehead in the only spot she did not have either a bandage or any noticeable burnt flesh. Isobel watched the two of them and was struck with a sudden rush of guilt as she turned to go. She never wanted to exit a room as badly as she wanted to vacate the Maguire's living room that day.

"I have to go," she said, "I have to make a few phone calls."

John gently said to her, "I'm so sorry about your husband."

Isobel felt like she had been punched in the stomach as she immediately regretted telling them she was going to make phone calls. Now she would *have* to tell Kim what happened to Tom. If she didn't, John would tell her and she would wonder why Isobel did *not* tell her.

Kim's attention, although slow, was reverted back to Isobel. "What happened to Tom?"

"You might want to sit back down for this," Isobel warned.

"No, I'll stand."

Isobel knew she had no choice but to tell her Tom was dead so, without hesitation, she said, "he died in an accident a couple days ago."

"What?" Kim asked, "What happened?"

Isobel found it hard to look at Kim when she spoke to her because her eyes kept drifting to the scars on her face. She couldn't help but wonder what it looked like under all of the bandages. She assumed those areas of Kim's face were worse than the exposed skin, otherwise; why would they be covered up? She finally spoke, "He crashed his truck."

Kim gasped and then groaned as if her sudden

breath was painful. "Oh my God! I'm so sorry," she cried as she cupped her left cheek in her hand (the left side of her face seemed to have gotten the brunt of the damage).

"Thank you," Isobel said, "are you okay?"

"Yeah. I just can't move my jaw too much because it feels like the skin is pulling."

"I'm so sorry," Isobel said. There was a lot of apologizing going on in the room.

Kim looked at Isobel and started to cry. "I'll be okay, I guess," she said as her nose started to run. She grabbed a tissue off the coffee table and dabbed at her eyes and nose. "You don't have to be sorry."

Isobel looked away from her face as she could not look her in the eye any longer. *If you only knew how responsible I am for what happened to you.* The thought was doing summer saults in her head as she searched for the right words to say. She absolutely did *not* want to discuss the matter any further in front of Kim's husband. It was going to be hard enough to admit it to Kim, but to confess in front of anyone else would be detrimental to Isobel's reputation around their community, or would it? *Who am I kidding? These people around here barely know me due to Tom's insecurities.*

Her brain was hurting as more and more thoughts flooded into it, so she took a shot and asked, "Can we have a moment alone?"

Kim looked at her with the most puzzled eyes as her eyebrows narrowed and she glanced at John as if she wanted him to speak up as to whether or not he thought it was a good idea. Then she looked away from him and back at Isobel. "Why?"

Isobel did not know exactly how to answer that question as she stood in her neighbor's living room feeling very awkward.

"John," Kim motioned to her husband, "I need some more bottled water. Would you mind going to get a case?"

Kim was instructed to drink lots of water to help with the healing process. The fact that she and John only drank bottled water was helpful to Isobel. His trip to the store would take at least half an hour which would be plenty of time for Isobel to admit the truth to Kim and for Kim to either freak out in hysterics or to simply throw her out of the house. Those were the two scenarios Isobel was getting mentally prepared for. She could not have prepared herself for what *actually* happened.

3 4

With John out of the house, Isobel seized her moment. She walked over to where Kim was standing and motioned for her gently with her hand telling her to sit back down on the couch. Kim looked down at the sofa cushion and then back at Isobel. She had no idea what was going on, but she was the first to speak.

"I don't want to sit. Something tells me I should stand for this conversation."

Isobel folded her hands in front of her, "I just thought you might be more comfortable," she said as she looked at the gauze covered face that was glaring back at her with only one eye.

"Actually," Kim said, "I would like a cup of tea."

"Let me get that for you." Isobel quickly responded. All she could see was the kettle of hot water spraying all over Kim's face. She had a clear vision of this in her head, even though she wasn't even there. She thought it was odd that tea was the first thing Kim wanted at that moment instead of just getting the conversation over with.

"I'm quite capable of making tea," Kim seemed offended.

"Oh, I know you are. I just wanted to help," Isobel lied. She did not trust Kim to make hot water after what happened. She had a quick thought in her head that her typing might not have a statute of limitations. The "accident" might keep happening.

Wait! That's crazy, right?

Kim walked into the kitchen with Isobel close on her heels. The medicine must have been wearing off because she seemed lucid and sturdy as she reached for the tea kettle and turned on the faucet. The kettle was a pretty hunter green color like the leaves in the stencils Isobel painted in her dining room a long time ago, that Tom never appreciated. Kim filled the teapot half-way with water, turned on the front burner of the stove, and placed the kettle on it.

"Kim," Isobel started the dreaded conversation, "I have something to tell you. I know we don't know each other very well, but..."

"Wait," Kim interrupted, "I know what this is about and I'm sorry."

Isobel was confused. "You do?"

"It was only for a short time and nothing happened," Kim tried to explain, "it was over before it started."

"What are you talking about?" Isobel was so ready to confess what she had done, but Kim had another agenda.

"Tom," she explained, "I'm so sorry about what happened."

"I know," Isobel said, "you already said that and I appreciate it."

"No!" Kim's voice rose, "I'm sorry about what happened between us. I want you to know that I never slept with him." She was calm now.

Isobel did not know what to say. How could she respond to this turn of events? She was not ready for this.

"He wanted to, but I refused," Kim continued. She started to cry as she reached behind her to search for a seat. She had become unbalanced.

Isobel stood there dumbfounded at the woman's unexpected confession. She pulled a chair out for Kim and helped her into it before responding to her statement. "You mean, you never...," she could not complete her question as images of the story she typed flashed in front of her eyes. She may have hurt Kim for nothing. The woman in front of her was probably going to have to bear permanent scars due to Isobel's jealousy when the only person to blame here was her husband, Tom. Well, she sure had taken care of him, hadn't she?

Kim blew her nose into a tissue as she spoke, "No. I could not do that to my husband, or to *you.*"

"Thank you," Isobel said, "for being so honest." She moved toward the door., and looked back in Kim's direction with the open door in her hand, "I'm sorry," she said before leaving to go back to her empty, cold house.

Kim wondered what Isobel was sorry about when she heard her husband's car pull into the driveway. They had ended their conversation just in time. She wanted to tell John about the affair she almost had, but then she thought, *what good would it do now?*

Isobel walked hastily across the Maguire's yard and into her own as she watched John walk into his house with a case of water. She wondered if Kim would ever tell John what they had talked about as she mulled over her decision not to add any more stress to their talk by adding in, *Oh! Bye the way, I made your accident happen by typing it on my typewriter!* It sounded so crazy in her mind and she just knew it would sound even more insane if she said it out loud.

The phone was ringing when Isobel got to her front door. She fumbled with the knob because her hands were shaking so badly from the weird conversation she just had with Kim, she was hardly able to hold onto it, but she got it open and ran inside, tripping over her interior door mat, the one that said, *Bless this house*, and almost falling flat on her face in a pile of glass that was still on the floor from her shattered glass of water. She was able to regain her balance just in time to grab the phone on its last ring, right before the answering machine would have picked it up. That was happening to her a lot lately with these phone calls.

"Hello?" She was out of breath and the other end of the line was silent. "Hello," she repeated.

"Mrs. Parrish?" There was a raspy sounding male voice on the line.

"Yes?"

"This is Bill Mathers from Clairemont Funeral Home. First let me say, I am very sorry for your loss."

Well, Mr. Mathers, I'm not sorry! "Thank you,"

"I have been contacted by the coroner's office regarding the release of your husband's body."

Why don't you get right to the point? Isobel was even angrier at Tom now that she knew he wanted to sleep with Kim. He didn't, but he *wanted* to. "Mr. Mathers, I don't want to be rude here, but they said he would not be released for about a week."

"That is true Mrs. Parrish," he said, "but they think he will be here by Friday"

Isobel didn't say anything.

"Are you alright, Mrs. Parrish?"

"Yes. I just wasn't ready to have to plan my husband's funeral."

"Yes, I'm sorry," Mr. Mathers consoled her. What he didn't realize was that Isobel was looking at the planning of Tom's funeral as an inconvenience, not a tragic experience.

"Thank you," she said, "Is it okay if I stop by tomorrow to get things started?"

Without hesitation, Mr. Mathers said, "Absolutely! I'll put you in for two in the afternoon. Is that okay?"

"Yes, that's fine," she said and she hung up the phone.

Mr. Mathers seemed to be a nice man, but Isobel could not stop thinking about her conversation with Kim the entire time she was on the phone with him. She made herself a note that said *2:00 funeral home* and put it on the refrigerator with the magnet she and Tom bought on their trip to Atlantic City seven years ago. That weekend getaway seemed like ages ago to her now as it was pre-beatings, pre-possessiveness, and pre-Kimberly Maguire.

Wait! You can't be mad at her. It was him!

Yeah, but she still flirted with him! She may not have slept with him, but she did not stop him from coming over.

No! Stop it! You have to fix this. She did nothing wrong...

As the argument continued inside Isobel's head she decided she needed to get out for a little while. She liked being home without Tom there, but; she was not ready to go back up to her cold bedroom. Actually, she was starting to feel cold downstairs now as well. She hoped it was just because the sun was going down, but she didn't stick around to find out. She grabbed a broom and dust pan and cleaned up the glass on the floor. Then she got a sweater from the coat closet by the front door, picked up her purse and keys from the table, and went outside to her car.

Isobel had heard of a little restaurant with home-style cooking like a diner, called Carrie's Cuisine. It was a little bit of a drive, but she wanted to get away, if only for a couple of hours. She got into her car and drove out of town.

The hostess sat Isobel at a quiet table in the corner. She was happy with her placement in the dining room as she could see the entire place. It was small and cozy, just what she needed that night. Then, she saw them. Carol from work walked in with a handsome gentleman who Isobel definitely knew. She had to get a better look at them as they walked across the dining room to their table before she could be sure, but she was right. It was Carissa's husband and they were dressed pretty fancy.

It was hard to enjoy her dinner after she saw them. *What is Carol doing here with him? More importantly, should I tell Carissa about this?* After finding out about Tom's almost affair, she knew Carissa had a right to know about this.

Isobel realized she hadn't been friends with the ladies from work for very long, so she suspected Carissa might not believe her. Just to be sure, she took her cell phone out of her purse and snapped a few photos of the date that was happening just a few tables away from her. She quickly put the phone back in her purse so she wouldn't get caught and she nervously flagged her waitress down so she could get her check. She didn't even finish her meal. She managed to barely make it out of the restaurant without Carol and Bill seeing her, but she did. At least, she *hoped* she did.

When she got home that night she went straight up to her room where it was still cold, but she dealt with it by putting on some warm pajamas and covering up with her thick comforter. She tossed and turned most of the night as the images of her coworker with her other coworker's husband would not leave her head. She managed to fall asleep just after four. Her alarm would go off an hour later.

Isobel woke up a few minutes before her alarm went off. She was shivering, even though she had her comforter on and she was dressed warm for bed. She sat up in bed, holding onto her blanket and glancing at her alarm clock. It was 5:49 am. She turned off the alarm, already awake, and that was when she noticed something was different about the table in her bedroom. The Royal was exposed and the white towel that was covering it was on the floor.

She got out of bed and looked at the towel, thinking that she may have put it there during the night. She was getting used to the strange happenings in her bedroom. Still shivering, she walked over to the thermostat and saw that it was set at seventy degrees, but it definitely was not that warm in her room. A chill ran up her spine as she turned around to put the towel back on top of the typewriter. As she gently draped it over the machine, she told herself she probably moved it while she was dreaming or something, but nothing would surprise her anymore about that typewriter after what it (*she*) had done to Kim and Tom.

Isobel went about that day like it was any other day. She was definitely not acting like a woman who just lost her husband and had to plan his funeral. She called the office to let them know she would not be in again, explaining that she had to go to the funeral home and make plans. That visit was pretty easy though. She met with Mr. Mathers, picked out a simple urn, and arranged to have Tom's body cremated. She wanted to be out of there as soon as possible. The Clairemont Funeral home gave her the creeps. She always wondered if there were dead bodies downstairs.

She quickly finished up her meeting with Mr. Mathers, hastily paid him, and signed all of the paperwork. There would be no funeral. Isobel had *other* things to deal with, more *important* things.

As she walked down the sidewalk in front of Clairemont Funeral Home, she remembered there was the small detail of Tom's life insurance policy, which she had completely forgotten about until that moment. At least *one* good thing would come out of her marriage.

Good riddance Tom!

Nice to know you Tom.

Fuck you Tom!

That evening was filled with sit-coms and wine for Isobel. She was starting to realize she could do her own thing without being punished. She did catch herself looking out the window a few times to see if she could get a glimpse of Kim, but Kim never so much as *walked* past any of their windows that night.

She decided she was probably better off *not* seeing Kim that night because she would just be flooded with guilt all over again. With a slight buzz from the wine, Isobel went to her bedroom to grab her pillow, and blanket, and some clothes to avoid having to go up-stairs to even change. She was going to sleep downstairs where the air was not so cold and her sleep would be uninterrupted.

Friday came and Isobel had not been to work since the beginning of the week. She knew her coworkers did not expect her back so soon after the tragedy, but they didn't know that she would much rather have been at work than home alone pretending to be devastated over the loss of her spouse. They also did not know of the ulterior motive she had to *want* to get back to work, but they would find out soon enough.

Isobel was driving herself crazy with her own thoughts whirling around in her head like a windmill. It was nice to not have Tom around, but she was realizing that she did not have any friends either, and she really *was* alone. She had slept in the living room the previous night because her room was becoming intolerable with its frigid temperatures and the typewriter she had not touched in days because it was starting to really freak her out. She even moved some of her clothes downstairs so she could get changed without having to go up *there*, up to her bedroom that she had become horrified of. The only thing she absolutely *had* to go up there for was to shower, which was what she needed to do that day because she was planning on going to the office.

As soon as Isobel started to climb the steps the landline in the kitchen started ringing, so she turned around, annoyed, and went to answer it. It was the state coroner.

"Good afternoon, Mrs. Parrish," he said, "I have your husband's autopsy report and, although I find it intriguing, it came back as inconclusive so the cause of death was likely a heart attack."

Isobel cleared her throat, "I don't understand. Why are you intrigued by this information?"

"Well," he started, "the man who was in the cab of the truck your husband crashed into stated that the vehicle was swerving back and forth on the highway before making a sudden turn into his truck."

"Couldn't a heart attack have caused him to be erratic?" she asked.

"Well, yes. I suppose it could, but the trucker said he had been driving that way for a long stretch of road."

"Oh." Isobel did not know what else to say at this point.

"We are ruling his death a heart attack," the coroner continued. "That is what will be on the death certificate. There were no marks on his body or any other damage internally that would tell us anything. His body was so clean. The only external markings were the ones left by the airbag, which deployed on impact."

"Okay, thank you," Isobel said.

"I just wanted you to know the details in case someone comes around asking you questions regarding this matter, However, I don't anticipate that. I am so sorry for your loss."

Isobel thanked him and ended the call after he told

her Tom's body will be released to the funeral home that Friday, just as Mr. Mathers said.

She started up the steps again to take that much-needed shower as the thoughts of the last few day's events started weighing heavily on her mind. She just wanted to get back into a normal routine (whatever *that* was).

As she showered and watched the previous day's events swirl down the drain, she thought of Kim again. What would she do about *that* situation? Kim was not the evil woman Isobel thought she was.

Isobel needed more time to think about how she was going to handle everything, so she called the office and told them she would be out until Monday. She would mull over the Kim situation all weekend with no hint of a resolution by Sunday night.

She decided to direct her focus on the problem she would face at work on Monday, the deceit that was happening right under Carissa's nose, the cheating...

Carol and Carissa were chatting and carrying on, telling each other about their weekend when Isobel walked into the office on Monday. They were at the coffee station, their usual meeting place. Isobel, trying to ignore the laughter between the two women who would soon become enemies, logged into her computer and immediately got to work, her phone already ringing. The ladies did not even see her come in as they continued their conversation obliviously.

Carol glanced over and saw Isobel at her desk. She tapped Carissa on the shoulder and nudged her head toward Isobel making a motion that they should go talk to her. They approached their coworker, hot coffee in hand, neither of them knowing exactly what to say as Isobel spoke on the phone with a client. She did not look like a woman who had just lost her husband. She hung up the phone and the women were standing in front of her desk.

Isobel broke the awkward silence. "Hi. Can I do something for you?"

Carissa spoke first. "We wanted to see if you were alright, and if you needed anything."

"I'm fine," Isobel said, narrowing her eyes at Carol. "Just anxious to get back to work."

"I can imagine," Carol said, trying to console her,

"but please let us know if you need anything. We are here to help you."

Isobel found this strange because Carol (except for that pizza lunch that she probably felt obligated to include her in) never gave Isobel the time of day.

Yeah, I'm sure you want to help me. Sorry Carol, but I don't have a husband anymore, so I have no man to offer you. Bitch!

"I'll be fine," Isobel said as she directed her attention back to her computer.

Carol and Carissa took the hint and walked away to start their own work days. It was Monday, which was always a busy day for them. They sat at their desks and started answering phone messages as Isobel wondered how and when she would approach Carissa regarding what she knew.

After an extremely busy morning, Carissa got up from her work station and headed for the door to go to lunch. Isobel noticed that Carol was still at her desk, so she took the opportunity to stop Carissa so she could talk to her. Isobel got up and almost had to run to the door to catch her. She caught up to Carissa as she walked outside.

She didn't want to give herself time to chicken out, so she stopped her immediately. "Can I talk to you for a minute?"

"I am really in a hurry," Carissa said, 'I'm sorry, I just have a couple of errands to run today."

"Oh," Isobel was disappointed, "I'm sorry, maybe later?"

Carissa noticed the urgency in Isobel's voice. "I wanted to get together with you anyway," she said, "outside of work."

Isobel started to turn away. She had nowhere to go for lunch. She packed a sandwich that day, but before she went back inside she turned back toward Carissa. "It can wait," she said, but Carissa continued to head toward her car, not catching what Isobel said.

As she returned to her desk, where she planned to eat her lunch, she heard Carol on her cell phone. She was laughing in that giddy schoolgirl way, and Isobel had a feeling she was talking with Bill. She directed her ear toward Carol's conversation. She wanted to be sure, so she would have a better chance of Carissa believing her, because now that she thought about it, she really had no reason to believe anything Isobel said to her. It wasn't like they were actually friends.

She couldn't quite make out the conversation, so Isobel walked over to the coffee station, which was within earshot of Carol's phone call. She didn't want coffee, but she took her time and brewed a pot just so she could hear that Carol was making dinner plans for the next evening. She heard her say something about going to their "usual" place. Isobel thought she knew where that was, and now she knew what she had to do.

Carissa was a little late getting back from lunch, and she jumped right back into her work, so Isobel did not have a chance to talk to her. She seized her moment when Carissa got up to get a soda from the kitchen. Humphrey's Homes had a small kitchen for the employees to eat and socialize in, though no one really ever used it. Isobel retrieved a dollar bill from her purse to make it look like she wanted a drink as well. When she reached the kitchen, Carissa was standing in front of the vending machine trying to make a decision about what she wanted to drink. Isobel walked up slowly behind her.

"Isn't it crazy how we look at the drink options as if it were a life or death situation?" she asked her coworker.

Carissa laughed. "You're right," she said as she looked at Isobel, "Are you really okay?"

"Yeah," Isobel said, "I'm hanging in, you know?"

"I'm so sorry about your loss." Carissa was sincere.

"Thank you." Isobel knew this was her moment. "Hey, what are you doing tomorrow night?"

Perplexed, Carissa looked at her. "Nothing, I guess. My husband always works late on Tuesday nights."

Sure, he does. If you only knew...

"Would you like to go out to dinner with me?" Isobel asked, "I'm tired of eating alone,"

"Sure," Carissa answered "But I would have to bring my daughter if that's okay."

Isobel wondered how the conversation would go with Carissa's daughter there.

What was her name? Oh yes, Chloe.

Not to mention, the place she was planning to meet her, the truth would come out without her having to say a word.

"That would be great!" Isobel had no idea how she was going to pull this off, but she would figure It out. "I know a nice place. It's about a thirty-minute drive from here, but it's quaint and the food is great."

Carissa agreed and they went back to work and finished out the day.

Carissa was getting ready to go out to dinner. She had no idea what to wear, but did she really have to worry about what she looked like? She was just going to dinner with Isobel, who she knew would not judge her. She put on a pair of jeans and a nice floral short-sleeve top. It was kind of warm that night, so she figured that she would be fine with a light jacket for when the sun went down. It always cooled off when the sun went down.

Chloe came into her mother's room and asked why she was getting dressed up. The outfit Carissa picked out was apparently not what she normally put on when she got home from work.

She turned around and smiled at her 14-year-old daughter. "We are going out to dinner with a friend of mine, so go get something nice on, okay?"

Chloe was all smiles as she went into her room and put on a blue blouse with ruffles around the bottom of its short sleeves. She got a white skirt and some brown boots that went up just above her ankles. Chloe always looked cute when her parents took her somewhere. When she was all dressed, she went back into her mom's room with her hairbrush and asked Carissa if she could put her hair in a French braid. Chloe had long blonde hair that she always had pulled up in some sort of way.

"Sure," Carissa said as she sat on her bed and patted her hand on the mattress next to her, telling Chloe to have a seat next to her.

Carissa's phone made a sound like a slot machine, which was her text message alert. She picked up her phone from the dresser, and saw that she had a message from Isobel.

I'll meet you at Carrie's Cuisine at 7:00. If you have any trouble finding the place, text me or call me.

They had exchanged phone numbers during their conversation at work. Carissa wondered why she never took the time to get to know the woman. Isobel seemed real nice to her; she just had a rough situation with her husband that she was always trying to cover up. She always felt sorry for her, but now she was going to have the chance to get to know her.

"Are you about ready to go Chloe?" Carissa asked as she finished with her braid.

"Yeah, Mom," Chloe was excited. She loved to go out to dinner and they haven't been doing that very much lately. "Where are we going?"

"A little place called Carrie's Cuisine," she answered.

The name sparked something in Chloe. "Oh, I've heard of that place."

"Oh, you have, have you?" she asked in a joking manner.

Chloe said, "yeah, I heard Dad talking about it once."

Carissa knew they had never been there, but she left it alone, assuming her daughter was mistaken. "Alright. If you're ready, let's get in the car and get going," she said, "I don't want to be late. It's a school night."

Chloe jumped up and fetched her mom's car keys from her purse and they got into Carissa's car and drove to the restaurant. It took them about a half hour to get there, just like Isobel said it would.

They pulled into a parking spot that was right by the front door. The restaurant did not look busy at all. Carissa and Chloe went in the door and the hostess greeted them immediately as there was no one else waiting.

Carissa quickly said to her, "We are meeting some-one here. It will be three of us."

Just as they walked over and sat on a bench in the lobby, obviously for people to use while they waited for a table, Isobel walked in. She spotted them on the bench, but she went to the hostess instead of going over to them first. She asked the hostess if they could sit at a corner table or a semi-private one.

Carissa saw her talking to the hostess and she and Chloe walked over to where they were standing. Isobel told her she had gotten them a table and they could sit down right away. As they walked to their table, Isobel scoped out the dining room to see if Carol was there yet. She didn't see her, so she hoped she heard her right and they were coming to the same place, or Isobel's plan would be shattered.

When they sat down, Carissa started the conversation. "You remember my daughter Chloe?" she asked.

"Of course," Isobel smiled at the teenage girl, "How are you dear?"

Chloe was all smiles as she fidgeted in her chair. "I'm fine." She was being shy, which Carissa thought was odd, because Chloe was usually outgoing.

"Well," Isobel changed the subject, "Are you hungry?"

"Yes," Chloe said. Now the woman was speaking her language.

The server came over to the table and introduced himself as Jeff. They ordered an appetizer because none of them knew what they wanted to eat for dinner yet. The heaping order of cheese fries with bacon would surely keep them satisfied until they made up their minds. That was their thought process anyway, however; when the fries came out they were all ready to order. Chloe ordered a cheeseburger while both women ordered fettuccini alfredo. Isobel told Carissa that this restaurant had some of the best fettuccini she had ever tasted as they dug into their appetizer.

They were seated in a booth that was surrounded on three sides by plants. Isobel could not see into the dining room very well, so she excused herself to go to the restroom so she could see if her plan could start being set in motion. She walked to the restroom and Carissa's husband was nowhere in sight, so she used the facilities and walked back to the table, but just before she made the turn to go to her table, she saw them. Bill and Carol walked in together with the hostess. Isobel waited until they sat down before she went to her table so she would know where they were sitting.

Their platters were being delivered as Isobel returned to the table. She contemplated how to go about her plan to expose Bill while they ate dinner. She knew she had some time because Bill and Carol hadn't even ordered dinner yet.

Chloe was the first to finish her dinner and she asked if she could go to the bathroom. Carissa said she could, and Isobel was so nervous the girl might see her father, but she returned to the table within five minutes and was ready to order dessert. Isobel took that opportunity to execute her plan.

"Why don't you go see if the hostess has a dessert menu?" she asked Chloe. She knew the hostess stand was in the opposite direction of her father's table. Chloe bounced up and left the table. Isobel knew she only had a second to play her card. "Carissa," she said softly, "Will you go over there and ask our server if I could have a glass of water? I'm not feeling too great," she lied.

Jeff was standing by the service bar getting drinks for another table when Carissa walked toward him. She would have to walk past the table her husband was entertaining another woman in order to get to the service bar. Isobel watched her walk halfway across the dining room, before she stopped suddenly and stared across the room. Isobel knew what she was looking at. Carissa quickly walked back to her table without the glass of water Isobel had requested.

Isobel didn't say a word when her coworker returned to the table. She thought it would be best to let Carissa have the first word about what she had just seen.

"I'm sorry," she said, "I couldn't get you the water."

Isobel did not want to play this game anymore so she just came out with it. "I'm sorry," she said, "I saw them here before and wanted you to see for yourself."

"So, you tricked me?" Carissa was angry.

"No," Isobel defended herself, "I thought that if I told you, you wouldn't believe me."

They ended their conversation abruptly when Chloe got back to the table. "I want chocolate ice cream," Chloe said.

Carissa grabbed her purse and jacket, "I don't think so," she said, "maybe another time Clo."

Disappointed, Chloe put her jacket on and thanked Isobel for having dinner with them. She was so polite. Carissa left enough money on the table to cover her meal and Chloe's meal and they walked out. Carissa did not look back as she hurried her daughter out the door so she wouldn't have to see her father with another woman.

The next day at the office was very awkward. None of the women spoke to one another. Even Carol and Carissa did not speak. Carol tried to approach her early in the day and was stopped short as Carissa made up a story about having a headache and wanting to be left alone. Isobel played it safe and didn't try to speak to either one of them, which wasn't entirely out of the ordinary for her as she had only just recently started talking to *anyone*.

The day was long and drawn out. It was only Wednesday, and the rest of the week would be torture if it continued the way it was going. When the end of the day finally came, after what seemed like forever, Carissa walked past Isobel's desk on her way out the door without looking back. Isobel quickly got up and tried to catch her, Carissa was in her car and was pretty much out of the parking lot before Isobel stepped out the front door.

"What's up with her?"

Isobel turned around to find Carol standing right behind her. "I'm not sure. I don't think she is feeling well". Isobel said, not wanting to tell Carol the truth.

Carol shrugged her shoulders and went back inside to get her jacket and purse with Isobel close at her heels. Both women gathered their belongings and left work for the day. They both felt like Carissa was mad at them, but for very different reasons.

Isobel's ride home took her right by the place Tom had crashed his truck and she found herself pulling over onto the side of the road where she knew the truckers stopped to rest. There was a designated area for them where the shoulder of the road widened to allow them room to stop.

Isobel pulled into the rest stop and there was one truck there with the cab door open. There was a man's leg hanging out of the door. It had faded blue jeans on and a light brown cowboy boot was dangling in the air. She knew the driver was not sleeping so she made herself scarce as she looked around for signs of her husband's accident.

As she studied the area where she knew the episode took place, she noticed there were no skid marks. She did see a large black spot on the blacktop surface that looked like motor oil or something had spilled or leaked out of someone's vehicle. She figured that was the exact area of impact. Even *she* knew that the lack of skid marks was usually a sign the driver had not stepped on the breaks or tried to stop.

Isobel got out of her car and walked over to the area where the spot was. A sudden chill ran through her body as she realized she stood in the place where her husband had lost his life. She felt herself get sad, only for a brief moment, before a smile overtook her face as her new reality came to light. She was free of that bastard!

She found herself doing something that was so out of character for her when she hocked up a really good full-bodied loogie and spit it out on the place he probably took his last breath. She had to give a brief giggle to herself before her eyes narrowed in both anger and satisfaction because she had the last word for once.

How do you like that, Fucker?

She got back into her car and drove away before the blue-jeaned trucker had a chance to see her. The rest of her drive home was a pleasant one. Her only worry now was what she was going to do about Carissa and Carol. She hated the fact that Carissa was mad at her. She had only been trying to help.

When she got home, she realized she was wrong. Carissa's anger toward her was the least of her worries as she pulled up her driveway and saw Kim sitting outside on her porch with Bentley. She was wearing a scarf over half of her face and Isobel wondered if that was going to be a permanent look from now on. She felt sorry for the woman who she used to loathe for messing around with her husband and for being beautiful. *Now look at her. Her life will never be the same because of my stupid jealousy.*

When Isobel got out of her car, Kim got up and went into her house. Her monstrous face was now something that kept her hidden away. Isobel was actually surprised to see her outside, even though it was brief.

With guilty thoughts weighing heavily on her mind, Isobel went into her own house where her clothes and personal items had taken over the downstairs.

She felt a cool breeze coming down the steps as she walked toward them. She was tired of living downstairs. She walked up the steps as if nothing out of the ordinary had happened up there. She was suddenly determined to face the evil that lurked within her bedroom, within the Royal.

When Isobel got to her bedroom (which she did without hesitation so she wouldn't turn around), the room was cold and the towel was still on the floor (instead of covering up the typewriter like she had hoped), but everything else was as she left it. She threw the towel on top of the typewriter and she went back downstairs to gather her belongings so she could move back into her own bedroom.

She started to think she really didn't have to be afraid of the Royal because she seemed to be in control of it, rather than the other way around. She realized that the terrible things that happened around her, only happened because she wanted them to. She *made* them happen. She typed stories on the thing and they came true!

The more she thought about it, the more she told herself that she did not have to be afraid. She was the one in control of her own destiny. But, how long would it take others to figure it out? How long would it be before someone linked her to the tragedies that were happening to people only *she* knew.

A sudden rush of paranoia came over her as her

mind desperately searched for answers as to how she was going to handle this. Should she get rid of the Royal? Should she get a different job? She wondered if she should distance herself from the people involved in the havoc her typewriter was creating.

Isobel didn't realize that she had managed to put all of her clothes back into their appropriate places while her mind was wandering in all directions. She turned away from her closet and walked over to the towel-covered typewriter and just stared at it as if she was looking through it. It was so quiet in her house as she stood mesmerized in her room; that was, until the phone rang and she just about jumped out of her skin.

She looked at the phone and just watched it ring, before finally answering it on the fourth ring. Out of breath and almost sweating, Isobel said, "Hello?"

PART II

The people of Hollow Creek were curious about the widow who moved into their neighborhood. She moved in to the only vacant house on Honeysuckle Drive and she had been there for at least a week before anyone saw her outside. She was constructing a garden in her front yard one sunny day and the sun cast a halo around her amazingly beautiful blonde hair.

It was Sergeant. Wright from the police station who first approached her to welcome her to the neighborhood. He was also her next-door neighbor which made her feel safe as soon as she moved in. The real-estate agent who sold her the exquisite house informed her of that fact when Isobel wanted a place to live where she would feel safe. She also chose the neighborhood because of its alluring attention to detail.

The home Isobel moved into was a charming three-story Victorian-style house that was painted the most captivating shade of red. It had black shutters, railings, and outside molding which outlined the house to give it added appeal. The houses around Isobel's were all beautiful in their own way, and no two looked alike. The manicured lawns that surrounded them looked like pictures out of a story book as sidewalks wrapped around them.

When Isobel got that phone call, the one that changed her life, she didn't look back. She had no idea

Tom had such a large life insurance policy and it was all hers. She never dreamed she would be able to quit her job at such a young age and buy her own place, one that did not have such brutal memories. She had finally unpacked everything after a week and a half. She had moved herself into the most attractive third-story bedroom where there was a single window, a walk-in closet, and a small sleeping area where she had her bed and a small dresser, not to mention the table that her typewriter used to sit on.

Isobel changed into a comfortable pair of sweats (she didn't mind wearing them now that she wasn't being forced to) when she was finished putting everything away. She poured herself a much-needed glass of Pinot Noir, but before she took a sip, she put the wine down on the table and went into her closet to grab a robe. It was a chilly night. That was when she saw it. She had forgotten that she set the box on the floor in her closet, the wooden crate with the Royal in it. It was the same box the typewriter was in when Arthur delivered it to her. It sat in the corner of her closet in the dark.

Isobel was in a new house in a new neighborhood. No one knew her here and she didn't know anyone, so what harm could it do? She opened the crate and slid it across the floor to where the table was. She knew she would not be able to carry it that far, but if she was able to get it right next to the table, she thought she might have a chance. She was barely able to pick it up, but she did manage. With everything in place, Isobel was ready to start her new life.

During the forty-five days she waited for the life insurance to pay out, Isobel decided to do some research on telekinesis and other forms of paranormal activity. She acquired a long list of books, reading each one from cover to cover. She kept them in one of her new rooms of her new home. She bought three book cases and filled them with books that taught her absolutely nothing about what she was going through with her typewriter.

Tired of reading, she decided to do some writing in her spare time (which she had plenty of now that she wasn't working). She always had a passion for writing short stories when she was younger, but Tom took that away from her with his way of always making her feel like she was not worth anything.

Isobel drove to the nearest department store where she knew she would be able to get some paper, as well as some other items she needed for the house. There was a Kmart about a mile away from her house, and it only took her a few minutes to get there. Hollow Creek was an easy town to get around in. Everything was centrally located on one main road.

She was in Kmart for only a half hour before she was standing in line at the check-out register. She had two reams of paper, a four-pack of Cottenelle toilet paper, and a light bulb for the lamp on her writing table. After she paid for her items, she went out to the parking lot to get into her car, when she heard the screeching sound of tires behind her. She turned around to see a blue Mustang with a rough looking driver with a scruffy face. He was hollering at Isobel.

"Hey lady," he yelled. "Why don't you watch where the hell you're going?"

Isobel stepped out of his way, but she could hear his continual yelling as he peeled out of the parking lot. Her heart was pounding in her chest as she made her way to her car. She got in and drove back toward her new home, completely on-edge from the confrontation in the Kmart parking lot.

On the way to Honeysuckle Drive, Isobel drove through a neighborhood where the houses were much smaller. They were nice, but smaller. She drove slowly through the neighborhood because the speed limit signs told her to only drive thirty-five miles per hour. It was a residential neighborhood with children playing outside in their yards. As she approached one of the homes, a rancher with a nice fenced-in yard, she noticed a woman getting out of a black car in the driveway. The woman looked very familiar to her and it wasn't until she was passing the house that she realized who it was. It was Carol Patterson. She was sure of it.

She drove past Carol and shielded her face so Carol wouldn't see her. When she got home she went straight up to her room with the paper and loaded a sheet into the typewriter. She wanted to get her mind involved in something else.

When she was all set up to write, she went downstairs to get a bottle of wine. She brought the whole bottle up so she would not have to keep traipsing up and down the steps to replenish her glass. When she got back to her room she was overwhelmed by cold air. She put her robe on and went over to her typewriter. She had planned a nice evening of typing and drinking wine. That idea was instantly taken from her when she looked at the typewriter and there was already a piece of paper loaded into it with one single word typed on it, which she *knew* she did not type.

H O W A R D

The bottle of Pino Noir slipped out of her hand and went crashing to the floor, splattering its blood-like color all over Isobel's new bedroom. Red wine dripped from every wall as spatters of it were splotched all over the ceiling and floor. Even Isobel was covered in it. Isobel's bedroom looked like a scene straight out of the Texas Chainsaw Massacre as she stood frozen in place. Wine dripped from her chin while her eyes remained glued to the paper, which only had a few droplets of wine on it.

The next morning, Isobel woke up in her bed and her room was clean. She had no recollection of anything after she dropped the wine the previous night. The only thing she remembered was the name Howard typed on the paper, which was still there. It did not make any sense to her. She didn't even know anyone named Howard, but now she knew that whatever entity haunted her before she moved was still with her and the typewriter now.

Not wanting to look at it anymore, she got out of bed and went downstairs to make coffee and watch the morning news, which she had become accustomed to.

The headlining news story was about a construction site accident, which claimed the life of one of the workers, who was a forty-one-year-old man. Isobel sat on her sofa and watched the story. The building the construction workers were working on had an unsecure area on the roof where, apparently, this man had been laying sheetrock. The other men that were around claimed to have not seen it happen. They just said that one minute he was up on the roof, and the next, he was on his back on the ground.

Isobel hated it when she watched the news and all they talked about was tragedy, so she decided to turn the TV off, but as soon as she aimed the remote control toward it to do so, the man's picture flashed up on the screen. Isobel swore it was the same man she had the run-in with at the Kmart. He looked exactly like him. Not only that, but he was standing next to a blue Mustang in the photo.

She didn't know what to do after seeing this. She thought the strange happenings might stop when she moved out of Clairemont, but if that was the same man, she knew one thing, she did not want to deal with this alone anymore. She had to tell someone and the only friend she really had was not talking to her. She needed someone so she just bit the bullet and made the phone call. She could only hope she wouldn't get hung up on as she apprehensively dialed the phone.

"Hello?" Carissa answered the phone as if she had just been woken up.

"Hey. Please don't hang up."

"Isobel?"

"Yes," Isobel was shaking as she spoke, "I wanted to get in touch with you and see how you are doing."

"I'm fine," Carissa said, "What happened to you? You just left work one day and never came back."

"I'm sorry," Isobel felt more at ease, "I didn't think you wanted to see me. I have so much to tell you."

"Let's do lunch." Carissa said invitingly.

"Okay," Isobel was surprised. "I moved out of town, but I'm not too far away. I'll come to you."

"My lunch hour is from one to two tomorrow. You want to meet me at Burger King?"

"Absolutely! I'll be there" She continued, "thanks Carissa. I thought you would still be mad at me."

"I know you've been through a lot. Tomorrow, then?" Carissa asked.

"Yes. I will definitely be there."

Isobel breathed a deep sigh of relief when she hung up the phone. The first part was finished. She made the call, which she realized was actually the easy part. Now she had to figure out a way to tell her friend about what has been going on, and that meant she would have to tell Carissa about Tom's death, about what *really* happened.

Isobel was nervous about her lunch date with Carissa. She hadn't seen her since she left Clairemont. She thought about her upcoming conversation with Carissa and how she would approach the topic of the typewriter the entire drive there. For that reason, she was thankful for the long ride.

She arrived at the Burger King fifteen minutes before her friend would get there. She used the restroom and found them a clean booth that was by a window. She sat at the table and anxiously waited until just a few minutes past one. Carissa walked in the glass door, where a bell jingled over-head announcing her arrival, just like the one at Humphrey's Homes, and she spotted Isobel right away. The restaurant was not very busy. There were only three tables that were occupied, theirs being one of them. Carissa went over to Isobel and they both walked to the register to order lunch.

With trays in-hand, the women walked to the condiment station to gather some napkins and ketchup before heading back to their booth. They both ordered the same thing: a cheeseburger, small fries, and a small Diet Pepsi. It was as if they ordered small meals so their lunch would not last longer than they were both comfortable with. Neither of them really knew what they were going to say to each other to rekindle a friendship that never really was a friendship to begin with. Isobel had a feeling that Carissa would run for the hills when she told her about the typewriter.

Carissa was the first to speak. "So, how have you been?"

"I've been okay. I'm getting by, you know? Moving was hard, but I needed a fresh start."

"I'm sure you did." There was a fly buzzing around the window next to them and it caught Carissa's attention. It was a welcome distraction.

"Look," Isobel said seriously, "I know you don't have long for lunch, so I'll get right to it." She looked down at the table to avoid making eye contact. "I'm sorry about what I did."

"It's over," Carissa interrupted, "And I'm alright. Just forget it, okay?"

Isobel looked up at her, "But it's not really over."

"What do you mean?"

"I didn't come here to talk about that night at the diner," Isobel said, "It's more complicated than that."

Carissa seemed to be getting agitated. "I know he is still cheating on me," she said, "But I have not confronted him about it because of our daughter."

"That's understandable," Isobel took a couple of her fries out of the pouch and ate them. "I need to share something with you," Isobel looked down again, "something I have been keeping to myself and now I have to tell someone."

Carissa looked puzzled as she listened to her speak.

It was as if a flood gate opened because Isobel started spilling the words from her mouth without thinking about what she was saying, and before she knew it, she had informed Carissa about the Royal typewriter and its evil doings, or *her* evil doings. She wasn't sure what was happening, but she thought it might stop when she moved away. What happened to the guy on the news could have been a coincidence, but the timing of it told Isobel it was not.

Isobel told Carissa about her neighbor Kim, who had to wear a scarf over her face now due to the burns that she knew she had caused. She told her about Tom and how she made him suffer before finally killing him. She told her about the names of people appearing on the blank pieces of paper and how strange things would happen to them. She even told her about the machine falling apart and putting itself back together.

Carissa did not know what to make of all of the information Isobel told her. She thought it sounded like a bunch of horseshit, but it was intriguing at the same time. It sounded like Isobel was making things happen to people who were not nice to her, or that she did not approve of. Carissa said nothing as Isobel continued with her story.

"On a couple of these occasions I think I blacked out," Isobel continued, "like the time I dropped the wine. I dropped wine on my bedroom floor and it went everywhere! I know it did because I saw it," she wasn't sure if she was trying to convince herself or Carissa that it actually happened, "but when I woke up the next morning, everything was clean. I don't remember cleaning it!" She was getting upset at that point.

Carissa reached across the table and grabbed her hand. "It's okay," she said. "We will figure it out."

Isobel liked that her friend said "we" as if this was no longer her problem alone. She started to cry and Carissa gave her a Kleenex she had in her purse.

"Where are you living now?" Carissa changed the subject.

Isobel dabbed her eyes and blew her nose before answering, "Hollow Creek. I was able to buy a nice place with Tom's life insurance money."

"Isn't that where Carol lives?"

"Yeah," Isobel said, "But I didn't know that until I saw her outside the other day."

Carissa looked at her watch, "I better get back to work, but maybe we can do this again. Maybe at your house? I would love to see it."

Isobel was glad she asked her friend to lunch. She felt much better about things now and it sounded like Carissa was going to help her deal with her situation, the Royal.

The women wrapped up their lunch and went their separate ways, but not before making plans to get together the following weekend. Carissa was to come over to Isobel's house on Saturday.

Saturday seemed to take forever to arrive as Isobel anxiously waited for it. She spent the morning cleaning because Carissa was supposed to get there around lunch time, which Isobel had completely prepared for. She made a tray of cold cuts with all the trimmings and she had a bottle of Chardonnay chilling for the occasion (she preferred red wine, but after the other night she wasn't taking any chances). She was a newbie at having company. Even when Tom was alive they never had anyone over to their house, so she was excited, but nervous at the same time.

Isobel was up in her room making her bed when she turned to look at the typewriter. She did not want it out in the open because it frightened her. She put it back in the wooden crate she had in her closet. She saved the original crate it was in when she bought it because there was nothing else the thing would fit in, and it came in handy when she packed up to move to Hollow Creek.

Just when she got it put away, the doorbell rang. It startled her, making her jump and bump her head on one of the racks in the closet. Putting her hand to her head, she walked out of the closet and downstairs to answer the door.

Carissa was standing at the door. She seemed to

be looking for something as she was staring down the street and didn't even notice that Isobel answered the door.

"Are you okay?" Isobel asked.

"Yes," she said.

"Please come in," Isobel opened the door and guided her into the foyer of her new home.

Carissa looked around in awe of the place as Isobel showed her around and gave her the grand tour. Carissa liked the Victorian style house, and offered her compliments the entire time, but the only thing she really wanted to see was the one thing Isobel did not show her right away, the typewriter.

The women went into the dining room where Isobel had set out all of the food and wine she prepared earlier that day. They enjoyed a nice lunch together before Carissa stood up abruptly. "So, where is it?" she asked.

Isobel knew exactly what she was talking about. "I didn't think it was a good idea to have it out."

"What do you mean?" Carissa's tone became angry. "That typewriter is the main thing I came here to see."

Isobel agreed and walked Carissa up to her bedroom where she had just put the machine away. It was so heavy, she didn't want to get it back out, but that wasn't a problem when Carissa saw it. She was more than willing to help Isobel get it up on the table so she could get a good look at it.

"So, you can make things happen with this thing," Carissa said.

"Well, I'm not sure exactly. All I know is that when I type on it, my typing comes true, but that's not all," she pointed to the blank sheet of paper that was in it. "The names I was telling you about?" she continued, "They are people who have wronged me in some way."

"So, this typewriter is a protector of *you*, so to speak?"

"I guess so, but I can't explain it." Isobel was beginning to regret inviting Carissa over to her house because it was getting real now. Carissa seemed curious about the machine, instead of scared like Isobel thought she would be.

Carissa put a finger to her chin and ran her other hand over the keyboard of the Royal as if she was absorbing each letter into her skin. She was engrossed in the mechanisms that put the typewriter together. It was as if Isobel wasn't even in the same room anymore; it was only Carissa and the Royal typewriter. The strangeness of it all made Isobel start to feel uncomfortable, almost jealous. This was *her* typewriter and now it appeared her friend was forming some kind of connection with it.

"Can I borrow it?" Carissa asked without taking her eyes off it.

Isobel hesitated, unsure of what to say. "Oh, I don't know if that is such a good idea."

Carissa looked up this time, "C'mon, it's not like I'm gonna hurt it or anything."

While Carissa waited for a response from Isobel, who was searching for a proper answer to give her, she

198

pressed down on a couple of the keys to see how the typed letters would look on the paper. It was only random typing, but she somehow managed to trigger the 'C', the 'A', and the 'R'.

Isobel finally found her voice, but was surprised at what came out of her mouth as she simply said, "Sure," with no enthusiasm at all. She didn't think anything of the fact that Carissa typed the word CAR on the paper.

Happy she was going to be taking the Royal home, Carissa suggested they put it back in the box and take it out to her car before returning to the dining room to enjoy the bottle of wine.

After the typewriter was secure in the trunk of Carissa's car, Isobel could not get it out of her mind that she was probably making a big mistake, the two women drank the entire bottle of wine (which was only two glasses a piece), while Carissa caught Isobel up on all the gossip around the office. That wasn't difficult since Humphrey's Homes was a small company. The biggest news was that Mr. Humphrey was dating again, and seemed to be happy. Carol, on the other hand, was complaining that her boyfriend might be seeing someone else.

Carissa looked at the floor and sighed, "if she only knew."

Isobel looked puzzled, "You haven't told her yet?"

"No," Carissa said, "and I don't plan to anytime soon. I don't want her to act weird around my daughter when I have her at the office."

"That's understandable," Isobel said.

They wrapped up their conversation at that point and said their goodbyes. Isobel made sure they made a plan to return the typewriter before Carissa pulled out of her driveway, and just like that, the visit was over. Isobel was alone again. Only this time, she was really alone; even her typewriter was gone.

She went inside and turned on the TV to keep herself occupied until she was ready to go to bed. With only a few shows to choose from, an old episode of *Unsolved Mysteries* was what she decided to watch. It was a boring episode so her mind had plenty of time to wander. She kept thinking about the few minutes she was with Carissa upstairs and Carissa's fascination with the typewriter. She kept wondering why it was so important for her to borrow it. *Wasn't she afraid of it at all? She touched it! She typed on it!*

Stop freaking out. It was nothing.

Yes, it was! It was something, I just don't know what!

Isobel continued to battle with herself. She thought she might be going crazy as these interior dialogues were becoming more and more frequent.

She typed on it!

It was only 3 letters, C A R! It was nothing, will you SHUT UP!

No! What was she typing? C A R... what? OH, MY GOD! C A R O L... She was typing CAROL!

Carol took her daughter Nikki to the Clairemont Mall. Nikki wanted a new pair of Sketchers. The two pairs she already owned were clearly not enough. She wanted the black ones with the purple logo and laces. They would go perfectly with her look of a distraught teenager. Nikki always dressed in dark colors and wore thick, black make-up, even though she was only fourteen years old. Her mom allowed her the freedom to dress the way she wanted as long as it wasn't too offensive.

They walked past all kinds of stores that no one ever shopped in anymore. There were numerous jewelry stores and a couple of kid's clothing stores before they started to get to stores Nikki was interested in: Hot Topic, Victoria's Secret (just for the bags), and Jersey's, which was where Nikki wanted to get her sneakers.

They went into the store and the shoes Nikki wanted were displayed on the wall to their left, just past the entrance. Nikki didn't waste any time before grabbing one of them off the shelf and flagging down one of the sales representatives. He was a nice gentleman who measured her foot for size and immediately went to the back of the store to their storage room to find her size. He was back in less than three minutes. Nikki tried them on, put her old sneakers in the box, and told her mom they were the ones. They fit perfectly and she wanted to wear them out of the store.

After paying for the sneakers, Carol suggested they grab a bite to eat in the food court. Their mall had a small food court that only consisted of a sub shop, a pizza place, a place that had pretty good burgers called Bumble's Burgers, and a Japanese restaurant. They got burgers and fries at Bumble's and sat at one of the tables in the court.

When they were just about finished eating, Carol started to gather up their garbage to take it to the closest trashcan. That was when she looked up and saw Bill standing in line for some pizza. She dumped her trash and started to walk toward him when he took his cell phone out of his pocket and answered a call. Carol didn't think much of it until she got close enough to him to hear his part of the conversation.

"I love you too," was all she heard Bill say and she quickly turned around and went back to her daughter.

"Nikki," she said, "We have to go."

"But I'm not finished my fries."

Carol grabbed Nikki's arm and snapped, "You can eat them in the car."

Nikki did not say anything. She just gathered her shopping bag and garbage from her meal, and got up from the table. Her mom never snapped at her like that. She wondered if she had done something wrong as Carol held onto her arm and guided her to the nearest exit out of the mall (which wasn't the same one they came in so they had to walk pretty far to get to their car). Carol did not want to risk Bill seeing them.

Once they were in the car and Carol was backing out of her parking space, she finally spoke. "I'm sorry hun," she said, "I just don't want to have you out too late on a school night,"

The ride home was rather quiet as Carol was completely preoccupied and Nikki just didn't know what to say. She managed to thank her mom for the sneakers, but that was the only conversation the entire ten-minute drive. Nikki was amazed at how long ten minutes could actually feel as she stared out the window in anticipation of getting home so she could get out of the awkward silence of the car.

Once they were in the driveway, Nikki jumped out of the car when it barely came to a stop. Carol parked the car and went into the house where she went to her room, leaving Nikki in the living room wondering what was wrong.

Carissa got to the office early on Monday. She had some unfinished projects from the previous week that she wanted completed early in the week. After typing up a report she kept putting off, she decided to return some phone calls. She had so many messages on her machine from over the weekend that it was going to take her all morning and part of the afternoon to call them all back.

She was not only getting phone calls from clients, but now that Isobel did not work there anymore, she also had to take care of secretarial things. Half of her messages that morning were regarding their company Christmas party. Carissa was in charge of booking the venue and entertainment, and she had sent out twenty-seven invitations, which people were starting to respond to. They always invited other real estate companies to join them.

She was so involved with a call she returned to a woman by the name of Leslie Woodrow, she didn't even hear Mr. Humphrey come in. He tapped her on the shoulder just to let her know he was there and she almost jumped right out of her skin, it startled her so much.

She put her index finger up to let him know she would be off the phone in a second and she motioned her head in a way that he knew she wanted to talk with him. He stood behind her until she finished up her phone call. She swiveled around in her chair and apologized to him because she hadn't made any coffee yet.

"It's okay, I've got it." He walked over to the coffee station to brew a pot of coffee. "Have you seen Carol?"

Carissa reached for her phone to make another call, but answered him first, "No, not yet."

Mr. Humphrey got his coffee cup out of the cabinet and added cream and sugar in it. "Huh," he kind of shrugged it off. "Maybe she's just running late this morning."

"Yeah, you're probably right," Carissa said before she dialed the phone number of a client she was supposed to show a house to that day.

The morning continued with no word from Carol and when it was almost eleven o'clock, Mr. Humphrey decided to call her cell phone. He normally wouldn't have waited that long to try to reach one of his employees that didn't show up for work, but he really thought Carol would walk in at any moment, and he was extremely busy that morning as he usually was on Mondays. It was their busiest day of the week.

The call went straight to voicemail and Mr. Humphrey left Carol a message asking her if she was alright and he asked her to please call the office. After the call, he started to get a little worried. He told Carissa that he left Carol a message and he was concerned about her. He thought Carissa's response to that was odd in that she really didn't respond at all. She just stood up and told him she had to go meet the Mulfords, who were interested in one of Humphrey's Homes' larger listings. Carissa was really hoping to make that sale. It was for a beautiful three-story home with an attached two car garage in the Meadow Lake development right off the main highway on the way into Clairemont. The consensus was that only people with lots of money could live there.

Carissa left the office to meet her clients, but her mind was on something else, something she couldn't tell Mr. Humphrey. As she drove the short distance to Meadow Lake, she noticed a disturbance on the side of the highway about a quarter of a mile ahead of her. There were dozens of blue, red, and, silver lights flashing, which she knew were a combination of police, fire, and maybe some rescue vehicles. She slowed down as she approached the scene and there was a man standing in the road directing traffic to turn left and take a detour.

Carissa was running late for her meeting, so the detour was not what she needed. She fished her cell phone out of her purse so she could call Mrs. Mulford and let her know she would be a few minutes late.

She looked away from the road for a second to dial her phone (she did not like the concept of Bluetooth) and when she looked back at the road with her phone to her ear, she slowed down to a crawl when she was able to see what was going on in the road.

It was the car that got her attention. She knew that car and she thought she knew what happened. She came to a complete stop in the road. The man with the bright yellow vest on was yelling at her to keep moving, and the guy in the car behind her was honking the horn of his Ford Taurus with ignorant impatience, but Carissa just stared into the middle of the scene in disbelief.

It can't be.

It was the sudden knock on her window that got Carissa's attention.

"Hey lady," Mr. yellow vest said, "You have to keep moving."

Carissa just nodded and gently edged her car forward to head into the detour. She couldn't believe what she had just seen. Should she call Mr. Humphrey? What would she say? She knew she shouldn't call him without knowing any specific details and without knowing if anyone was hurt. It would only cause him to worry more.

Unanswered questions circled in her head as she approached the house where she was to meet her clients. She pulled into the driveway and opened her car door. She was just stepping out of her car when her cell phone rang.

Carol was getting ready for work after a weekend of continual crying because of the partial conversation she heard from Bill on his phone. Her suspicion was confirmed, he was seeing someone else. He had tried to call her three times on Sunday, but she did not answer. She did listen to his messages of lies telling her how much he missed her and couldn't wait for their date on Tuesday night at their usual spot. She didn't bother returning any of his calls, and she sure as *hell* was not going on that date anymore. Not now, not *ever*. now that she knew he obviously had some other woman on the side.

She didn't bother with too much make-up Monday morning because she figured it would just run all over her face if she decided to cry some more.

Her drive to work was much-needed therapy as she had forty-five minutes to be alone with her own thoughts and there was no one asking her what was bothering her every five minutes. She loved her daughter but there were some things she was too young to understand.

She was just pulling out of her neighborhood when she got a sudden itchy feeling on her right forearm, which sucked because it happened right when she had to downshift (she was one of the few people who still drove a stick shift) as she approached the intersection where she had to turn. She came to a complete stop at the stop sign so she could scratch it with her other hand.

It was a chilly morning so she had a jacket on, which she tore off her body as if it were on fire. She dug into her bare forearm with her nails for several seconds before the itch finally subsided. She continued her journey to work until she got to the highway that took her all the way into Clairemont. Her arm had a subtle burning sensation in the spot she scratched. She figured she probably dug her nails into her skin too hard and the burning would subside. She couldn't have been more wrong.

Carol looked down at her arm as the burn turned into a sting. She felt a sharp, nagging stinging pain deep within her skin and she had reached an area of the highway where there was no place to stop. She thought she would stop at the next drug store and get something to make her arm feel better. She had no idea what she would get since she had no idea what the problem was. She just wanted it to go away, but it was only getting worse.

Her arm started to itch again on top of the burning and stinging, so she let go of her steering wheel in order to scratch it. Her fingernails were offering no relief to the itch this time so she continued to dig into her skin until she noticed the blood on her fingers. Her forearm was bleeding. She had scratched herself so hard that she broke through the skin.

What the hell? She thought as she noticed she had drifted into the passing lane of the highway and traffic had picked up to the point she would not be able to switch lanes and pull over on the side of the road. She continued to drive, scratch, and now she was yelling because the pain had become excruciating.

Carol's entire forearm began to turn a deep color red as it swelled right in front of her eyes. She could actually see it getting larger as she prayed for a break in the traffic.

Finally, there was a break in the lane next to her just big enough for her to get into, but when she tried to reach her arm up to the wheel in order to swerve into it, her arm would not move. It was as if it was paralyzed. Carol thought, for one brief second, she wished it was paralyzed because then she wouldn't feel the unbearable pain that had taken over her entire arm.

With her good arm, she was able to pull into the slow lane where she actually spotted an area in the shoulder, just ahead of her, where she would be able to pull over. The only problem was that her dead arm was stuck on the gearshift.

With a car closely tailing her from behind and another one just off the tip of her bumper in front of her, Carol took her left hand off the steering wheel and reached it over the front of her body to move her other hand off the gearshift, but froze at the sight she saw.

Carol screamed bloody murder as she watched the

skin of her arm move as if something was under it trying to get out. Her arm pulsated like a cocoon of baby spiders as she continued to scream and drift off the side of the road, not paying attention to where she was going.

The throbbing, pulsating appendage continued to swell until a small incision-like opening began to form on the inside of her forearm. Carol continued to scream as her arm began to open and spill blood everywhere. The car was finally on the shoulder of the road and Carol, unable to down shift, slammed on her breaks. The car made a loud screeching sound as it came to a jolting stop. It was so loud Carol did not even notice the clunk and thump that happened as if she had run over a speed bump at full speed.

On the side of the road, her nightmare was not over. The blood leaking from her arm had begun to spill again as she looked down at it and saw something underneath it. She also heard a humming noise that sounded like a low tone on a kazoo, which was getting louder by the second.

Carol desperately tried to open her car door with her good hand, but it would not budge. She couldn't get out and she had no idea what was happening to her as traffic continued to pass without stopping to help her.

The forearm cocoon continued to burn as she saw something come out of it. Something had flown out of her arm and was buzzing around the windshield. She looked at her arm in disbelief, and more of the same flew out. Before she knew it, dozens of insect-like things were buzzing around the inside of her car and she could not get out. They were covered with her blood so she could not tell what they were until one landed on her hand.

"FUCKING BEES!" she screamed as she batted her fists in the air to wave them away from her face.

Buzzing bees continued to fly out of Carol's arm and swarm around the inside of her car as she frantically beat on her window. She knew her only escape would be to break the window and climb out of the car since the door handle would not budge.

The inside of her car looked like something out of a Stephen King movie and her arm looked like it had been through a meat grinder when her car door finally opened. She continued to scream uncontrollably as a man pulled her out of her car. She fought his grasp and broke free from him only to walk into oncoming traffic.

The man tried to call her back as a small pick-up truck came to a screeching halt, just inches away from her. Seeming to not notice any of this, she just held her arm out in front of her. The driver of the truck got out and directed Carol back to the side of the road. That was when she noticed all of the emergency vehicles.

Carol slowly came to as a young paramedic snapped his fingers in front of her, "Lady, are you alright?"

Her blurred vision returned as she reached for her arm and began to scream. "DON'T YOU SEE IT?"

The young man's look of sympathy and confusion made it clear that he had no idea what she was talking about. He waved for his partner to come over. Carol was sitting on the back ledge of their ambulance when she pulled her arm up in front of the young man's face. She looked distraught when there was nothing but a normal looking arm in front of him, and her.

"I swear," she cried, "It was cut open and...and..." Her hysterics made it impossible for her to explain what happened.

She was only able to get bits and pieces out, but it was enough for them to put her on a gurney and load her into the ambulance. The paramedics knew she had to be in shock because she was going on about her arm and pointed to it, but they didn't see anything wrong.

They left her in the back of the ambulance with the back doors open and she could see men and women rushing around outside. She saw a second gurney get wheeled behind the ambulance she was in as the men who were pushing it rushed it into the back of a second ambulance. There was someone else on that gurney and, for some reason, everyone seemed more attentive to that person than they were to Carol.

While Carol waited for someone, *anyone*, to come back to her, she pulled her arm out from under the sheet. Surprised that she was able to move it, she looked at it and it looked normal. There didn't appear to be any evidence of any trauma to the arm that almost caused her to kill herself a moment ago.

A couple of police officers got into the back of the ambulance with Carol as the paramedics loaded their gear and headed to the hospital with the second ambulance closely behind them.

The woman officer spoke first. "Can you tell us what happened, Ms. Patterson?"

Carol was scared. She didn't want to tell them the truth because she knew how crazy it sounded. As it turned out, she didn't have to explain the horror that was her arm because the paramedics already filled the police in on her story. She didn't say anything as the police woman wrote something down on her notepad.

"Did you know the victim?" the police woman asked.

That got Carol's attention. "Victim?"

"Yes," Ms. Police woman said, "the one you hit with your car."

Carol was mortified. *Hit with my car? What do they mean? I didn't hit anyone!*

Just then, Carol's mind went back to the moment her car came to a screeching halt. She felt a thump.

OH, MY GOD!

WHAT DID I DO?

She knew she would have to explain herself now. There was no way around it, so for the next ten minutes (which was the rest of the ride to the hospital) words just poured out of her mouth as she frantically tried to explain what happened with her arm while she was driving. The officers didn't say anything while she spoke. They just wrote lots of notes in their little note pads.

She told them about the pain. She told them about the terrible itch. She told them about the swelling, and the open wound on her arm, and the bees. She told them about the bees!

Oh, my God, the bees!

Did they see the bees?

Carol was relieved when they got to the hospital. She wanted to get out of that situation with the cops. Her gurney was taken over by hospital staff as soon as they arrived. She was wheeled through several hallways and right into a room, where they transferred her from the gurney to a hospital bed.

"The doctor will be in with you shortly," a cute blonde nurse said to her as they left her alone in the hospital room.

Carol did not know what was going on with her. She wasn't hurt (not that she knew of anyway). At least not that anyone else could see. She stewed in the bed for a few minutes before a doctor came in and introduced himself as Dr. Davis from the psych ward.

Psych ward? What the hell am I doing in the psych ward?

He explained that she was there due to some hallucinations that caused a horrific fatal car accident. She tried to explain to him that she was not in an accident because there were no other cars involved with her incident. He listened to her explain her case before filling her in on the part she obviously did not remember.

"Ms. Patterson," he said as he placed his hand on hers, "You hit a pedestrian with your car."

Carol broke into hysterical tears and cried out, "Are they alright?"

Dr. Davis looked down at the floor. He couldn't even look her in the eye when he said, "Unfortunately, she did not make it. They are working on finding out her identity now."

Carol just wanted to be alone at that point, so she asked the doctor to leave. He showed her where the call button was for the nurse if she needed anything and he left the room.

Later that evening, a nurse came into Carol's room to check her vitals and Carol asked her to turn on the TV. She also asked how long she had to stay in the hospital. The nurse apologized for not knowing the answer to the question, but she promised to find out as she found a news program on TV that Carol wanted to watch.

The top story of the evening news was about her accident. There was a reporter at the scene who explained what happened the best she could while Carol's car sat in the background of the picture. The woman pointed to the center of the road as her cameraman directed his camera there and she talked about the woman who was hit and killed.

"Witnesses said Liz was walking on the shoulder of the road looking at her cell phone, not paying attention to anything around her. She never saw the car coming," the reporter said.

Carol couldn't watch anymore. She grabbed the remote off the table next to her and turned it off as she rolled over and tried to fall asleep.

Carissa returned to the office after showing the house to Mr. and Mrs. Mulford. The appointment with them was a blur in her mind because she had been so distracted when she was supposed to be telling them the good points of the house and the neighborhood. She could not get the scene from the highway out of her head, and she knew she had probably blown the sale.

She did not say anything to Mr. Humphrey about what she saw because she wasn't absolutely sure it was Carol's car. When he asked how her appointment went, she assured him everything was fine and promised to call the clients in a day or two to see if they wanted to go ahead and get the paperwork started. To her boss, she made it sound like she made the sale.

The rest of the day at work went by slowly. Carissa didn't think she was ever going to get out of there. It didn't help that she was really anxious to get home and pack up the Royal. After what she had seen that day, and what she suspected, she wanted to returned that damned typewriter to Isobel as soon as possible.

She thought she had done what she planned on doing with it, but now she wished she could take it back. She didn't really believe the stories Isobel told her about the Royal, until now.

Five o'clock finally came and Carissa was out the

door before Mr. Humphrey even knew what time it was. She didn't bother to say goodbye to him. She just wanted to get home.

She violated all kinds of traffic laws so she could get home as quickly as possible. She paid no attention to the speedometer as it passed seventy-five miles per hour. Highway eighty-four was usually littered with cops, but not on that Monday. It was smooth sailing all the way home. She didn't even hit any of the rush hour traffic. She left work so quickly and was able to get on the road ahead of that ruckus.

When she got home, her intentions, as well as her car, came to a screeching halt when she saw her daughter sitting in the driveway crying. Chloe was sitting with her legs crossed Indian-style with her face buried in the palms of her hands. Carissa parked the car and quickly got out to attend to her.

Chloe was fourteen, the age when every little thing was the end of the world, but usually not for her. She was not like most girls her age. She was a "Mama's girl" right from the beginning and she was usually so happy.

It was chilly outside, so Carissa convinced her to go inside where they could talk. Chloe told her mom that her father had come home and rushed back out the door before Chloe could show him her report card. She had been excited to show him when he got home, but he said, "Not now," and left without telling her where he was going.

"May I see your report card?" Carissa asked.

Chloe walked into the next room and pulled it out of her bookbag. She handed it to her mother as she looked down at the floor.

"This is wonderful honey!" Carissa wrapped her arms around Chloe and kissed her on top of the head as she held the piece of paper in her hand that reflected six A's and one B for the marking period. "This calls for a celebration, don't you think?"

"Can we go get ice cream tonight after dinner?" she asked as a single tear dried on her right cheek.

"Absolutely," Carissa said, "I just have to do something first."

Chloe turned and went to put her report card back in her bookbag while Carissa put her purse and keys on the counter and headed to her bedroom where she intended to put the Royal back in its box. She was going to put it back in her car so she could return it.

When she reached the door of her bedroom, which was closed because she didn't want Chloe messing around with the typewriter, she opened it and was immediately horror-struck as she entered the doorway.

What the hell?

Where is it?

Carissa started shaking as she frantically rummaged through her room, totally panicked at the sight in front of her, or rather, what was *not* in front of her. The Royal was gone.

Isobel got home from work a little late. When she left Clairemont and moved to Hollow Creek, she found a part-time job at the local library. She loved books, and now she could be around them all the time. Her job was simple; she was in charge of returning all of the books to their appropriate places on the shelves when people returned them. She usually only worked on Tuesdays and Thursdays, but the head librarian needed help with a project that Monday and Isobel welcomed the extra hours.

She was tired when she got home, and all she wanted to do was change into something comfortable and take her shoes off. She had to dress nice for the library so she usually wore high heels. The only other thing she wanted to do that evening was call Carissa. She wanted to know whether or not she had used the typewriter yet, and if she experienced anything strange afterwards. She also wanted to know if the machine had done anything eerie on its own as it sometimes did.

Isobel went straight into the living room when she got home. After literally kicking her shoes off so forcefully that her left one flew straight up and landed on the coffee table in front of her, she rubbed her feet for a few minutes. Her job required her to be on her feet for most of the day, and she was developing a blister on her big toe that was becoming bothersome.

While she was sitting on the sofa she noticed her purse on the floor next to the coffee table, right where she dropped it. Knowing her cell phone was in there, she bent over and picked it up. She fished out her phone and hit the on button to light up she screen. Then she touched the picture of the phone on her touchscreen so her contact list would display. Carissa's name was right at the top because she was the last person Isobel had called. In fact, she was the *only* person Isobel had called in a long time.

She lightly touched Carissa's name with her finger and waited for the robotic ringing sound that is characteristic of cell phones.

The phone rang one full ring and Carissa answered the line halfway through the second ring. "Hello?" She was out of breath like she had just finished an aerobics class, "Is that you, Isobel?"

"Yes. Is everything okay?"

"Were you at my house today?" Carissa asked.

Isobel was confused. "No. Why would I be at your house?"

"DON'T *LIE* TO ME!" she shouted.

The raise in Carissa's voice concerned Isobel. "Calm down. I was at work all day. Tell me what happened."

Carissa cried as she took a couple of deep breaths, "the typewriter," she hesitated.

"What is it?"

"It's gone," she almost whispered.

"What did you say?" Isobel heard her but did not believe her.

"GONE!" Carissa yelled.

Isobel didn't say anything for a few seconds to allow herself to gather her thoughts. "When?" she said, "I mean, how long ago did you notice it was missing?"

"When I got home from work," Carissa answered.

Isobel started to head up to her bedroom as she tried to console Carissa. "Did anyone know you had it?"

"No. I don't think so."

"Okay, calm down," Isobel said. "I'm going to get changed and come over. We'll find it." She said this, but she wasn't too sure.

"Alright, but hurry," Carissa was scared.

Isobel lightly pushed her bedroom door open, "I wi...," as she stood in her doorway, dropped her phone, mouth gaping.

Carol heard a buzzing noise coming out of the closet in her hospital room. For a moment, it took her right back into the hell that was the swarm of bees in her car. She snapped out of that scene and realized her purse was in the closet, so it must have been her cell phone that was making that sound.

She hit the call button for the nurse. When no one came in, she proceeded to get out of her bed by herself. She had only waited five minutes, but it was more than enough time for her to miss the call. She wanted to know who it was and she wanted someone to rescue her from the hospital. She didn't know why they were holding her there. She knew they didn't believe her story.

But, can they really keep me here?

They think I'm crazy! That's right, just your ordinary psycho! Of course, they can keep me here.

Someone had hung her clothes and her purse neatly on hangers in the closet. She assumed it was the nurse. She reached into her purse and felt her phone on the bottom of it amongst a bunch of loose change. She always seemed to accumulate lots of change in her purse, which made the thing feel like it weighed twenty pounds.

The screen on Carol's phone said she had missed a call from Nikki. She got a little freaked out because she knew her daughter was probably worried sick about her. She was never home from work late unless she called to let Nikki know. She hurriedly touched the keypad and found Nikki's name so she could call her back, but she had no idea what she was going to say to her.

"Hey Mom," Nikki answered right away. "Where are you?"

Carol searched for something to say. "I ran into a little trouble. I might not make it home tonight."

"What do you mean?" Nikki sounded upset. Carol never left her home alone over night before.

"I had some car trouble. I am at Clairemont Hospital."

Nikki cut in, "On my God! Are you okay?" She almost shouted.

"I'm fine, hun," Carol lied, "I am not sure when I will be home."

"Don't worry about me Mom," Nikki was upset. "I just want you to be okay."

Carol looked at the doorway to her hospital room as she heard someone come in. It was her nurse. "I will be fine," Carol reassured Nikki, "Do you want me to call your father? He will come there if you need him."

"No," Nikki was quick to answer, "I will be okay. Just keep me posted."

They both said they loved each other and they ended the call. Nikki had a good relationship with both of her parents, but she knew her father worked very hard and she did not want to disturb him just to come home and babysit her. She was plenty old enough to take care of herself.

Carol asked the nurse how much she knew about her accident, or the woman who was killed.

The nurse claimed to not really know anything but what was rumored around the hospital, and she assured Carol she was not one to help spread rumors.

"Can you send Dr. Davis in?" Carol asked, "I would like to talk with him about my discharge."

"I'm sorry," the nurse said, "He has left for the evening."

"You mean I have to stay here?"

"I'm sorry, but I don't have any orders to discharge you at this time."

Carol started to cry, "But, they have it all wrong," she cried, "I didn't have any hallucinations!"

"That is something you have to work out with your doctor." The nurse filled Carol's water pitcher and left the room, leaving Carol alone with her thoughts.

Carol knew what happened to her in her car, but she could not tell anyone the truth because they thought she was crazy. The thing that bothered her the most was that she hit and killed someone while she was fighting with the bees in her car.

She sat on the edge of her hospital bed and realized how crazy that sounded.

"Isobel," Carissa said into the phone, "Isobel, are you still there?"

Nothing on the other end of the line.

"Hey," she tried again, "Isobel,,," nothing, "ISOBEL!" She screamed into the phone.

Still, not a sound was heard on the other end.

Carissa hit the 'end call' tab on her phone and raced to the kitchen to get her car keys. She was going to drive to Isobel's house as fast as she could because something was clearly wrong. She had no idea where the typewriter was and now, something might have happened to Isobel.

Carissa grabbed her purse and ran out of the door with her phone still in her hand. She got into her car and started her journey to Hollow Creek. The drive was long enough for her to think about her botched appointment for work, Carol's accident (or the one she *thought* Carol was in), her husband's affair with Carol, and the Royal.

Oh my God! The Royal; where the hell is it?

She thought Isobel was going to be mad at her for losing it. The only explanation she could come up with was that someone must have stolen it, but, who? She couldn't figure out who could have possibly known about it, let alone, wanted to *steel* it.

I mean, c'mon... The thing must be a thousand years old for Christ's sake!

She tried to clear her mind of all of the bullshit that had happened over the past week so she could come up with a way to break it to her new friend that she lost her typewriter. No good story came to mind, and before she knew it, she found herself in Isobel's neighborhood. She was out of time. She would just have to tell her the truth, which was that she had no idea what happened.

She pulled up into Isobel's driveway, got out of her car, and went to the front door and rang the doorbell.

No one answered.

Carissa rang the bell again and waited a few more seconds.

Still, no answer.

She reached for the doorknob and found it unlocked, so she slowly pushed the door open and stepped into the open foyer at the bottom of the stairs. The house was eerily quiet. The only sound Carissa heard was the echo of her own heels on the hardwood floor. She still had the same shoes on she had worn to work that day. She could see the living room and the kitchen from where she stood. Isobel's Victorian house had a beautiful open floorplan.

Carissa did not see Isobel downstairs, so she started to climb the steps. There was no one on the second floor either, so she went all the way up to the third floor, where she saw the hallway that she knew led to Isobel's bedroom. She slowly approached the room. She was nervous as to what she might find on the other side of the door, which was open just a smidgen. She walked to it, shivering the entire time as it was unnaturally cold up there. She did not remember it being chilly downstairs, but then again, she was nervous so she convinced herself that anything was possible.

As the partially opened door drew nearer with each step, Carissa's heart pounded so hard in her chest, she thought it would come out of her throat. She reached for the door when she was close enough to it. With her fingertips, she gently pushed the door so it opened just enough for her to see her friend sitting on the bed with her hands folded in her lap.

"Isobel," Carissa whispered her name.

Isobel's head jerked and she looked straight at Carissa. "Do you see it?"

"Do I see what?" Carissa proceeded to look around the room until her gaze stopped dead. "Oh my God!"

"Did you return it while I was out?" Isobel asked.

"N...No!" Carissa could hardly get the word out as she wondered how the hell the typewriter had gotten back to Isobel's house.

Isobel gave Carissa a hard look as she narrowed her eyes and asked, "What did you do?"

"What are you talking about?"

Isobel just pointed at the Royal, which had a piece of paper in it.

"I didn't do anything," Carissa tried to defend herself, but she was confused and scared. "I mean... I wanted to, but..."

"BUT WHAT?" Isobel screamed.

Carissa hesitantly tried to speak, but the anger in Isobel's voice scared her.

"You better start talking!"

Carissa looked at the Royal. "I was mad at her because of what you told me. I thought I could...," she stopped.

"I told you the stories. I told you what this thing could do." Isobel was angry, "You should have just left it alone."

Carissa started to cry as they both walked over to the machine and looked down at the single word that was typed in capital letters.

C A R O L

Carissa, then started to tell Isobel about the accident she had seen earlier that day and how she thought it might have been Carol's car on the side of the road. As she spoke, the two of them noticed there were some keys missing from the typewriter's keyboard.

Isobel ran her hand along the holes where the letters should have been just to make sure they were not stuck inside the keyboard somewhere. Realizing they were actually missing, she shook her head. "What the hell..."

Both women stood with their hands on their hips in total confusion and amazement as they took note of the L, I, and Z as the missing keys. Before they had time to try to put their heads together to figure out what happened to the three keys, the doorbell rang, startling them. They both jumped and bumped shoulders, which diverted their attention from the bizarre happenings that were right in front of them, and forced a much-needed giggle session.

"I guess I better get that," Isobel said.

Carissa followed close behind her as she went all the way downstairs to answer the door. There was no way she was going to stay upstairs all by herself. The women reached the door and when Isobel answered it, she could not believe who was standing on her front porch.

"Mrs. Parrish?" The young girl at the door looked a little skittish as she addressed Isobel.

"Hello," Isobel said as she remembered her face. "Are you okay?" She knew it was Carol's daughter Nikki who stood in front of her, but she had no idea why she would be coming over to her house.

"I'm okay," Nikki said, "I just wanted to ask you about your typewriter."

All of Isobel's nerves went into shock when she heard that word come out of Nikki's mouth. How did she know about the typewriter and what could she possibly want with it? Isobel stepped out onto the front porch with her right foot, just far enough to take a wandering glance around the area to make sure no one could hear the conversation. She saw no one, but decided to invite the teenager inside anyway.

"What are you talking about hun?"

Nikki stood with her hands folder in front of her. "My mom told me about your typewriter," she said, "and what it is capable of."

"What do you mean, capable of?" Isobel asked.

Nikki noticed Carissa standing there and nodded in acknowledgement of her. "Mom is in the hospital."

"What?" Isobel asked.

"She said she had car trouble, but I think she was

in an accident," Nikki stopped abruptly, but it was obvious she wanted to say more.

"I'm sorry, dear," Isobel said, "is she alright?"

"Yes," she said, "at least I think she is."

Isobel knew she had to get Nikki out of her house so she and Carissa could figure out their own dilemma. She took her by the elbow and started to direct her toward the door. "Please let me know if you need anything," she said as she opened the door to hint she wanted Nikki to leave.

"Oh," Nikki smirked, "I will."

Nikki walked out the door and away from the house without another word. She saw the neighbor boy come outside to check the mail. She knew Kenneth from school. He was the son of Sergeant Wright of the Hollow Creek Police Department.

"Hey Nikki," Kenneth was always so friendly, "How's it going?"

"Alright," she said as she continued to walk right past him without stopping, or even looking at him. She just looked down at the sidewalk as thoughts of her weird encounter with Mrs. Parrish haunted her head.

The Pattersons lived a couple of blocks away from Isobel. The neighborhoods were completely different though. Once Nikki turned off Honeysuckle Drive and onto her road the houses changed from the huge, luxurious Victorian-style homes to one story ranchers, some with garages, and some with only driveways that had walkways leading to their front doors. The neighborhood was quaint with freshly mowed lawns.

Nikki arrived at her house where her dog Buddy, was anxiously waiting for her, his nose pressed up against the front window that overlooked their yard. The moment she stepped into the house, she grabbed his leash and took him outside for a short walk so she could gather her thoughts as to what her next move would be. She knew that both Isobel and Carissa wanted her to leave. They had no intentions of helping her out by giving her any information, which only made Nikki more suspicious that something sinister was going on. Her mom was in the hospital and she knew it had something to do with that stupid typewriter. She only wanted to look at it.

What would the harm be?

It didn't matter. Nikki would get her turn. All she knew was that her mom had been upset lately and she knew it had something to do with Bill, who she wasn't even seeing anymore, Isobel, who didn't even work at the same office with her mom anymore, and Carissa, who she suspected was the woman responsible for her mom's break-up with Bill. She thought they were probably just blowing her off because she was just some stupid teenager in their eyes, but she would show *them!*

"What do you make of that?" Isobel asked Carissa.

"I'm not sure," Carissa said, "She obviously knows about your typewriter."

Both women went back upstairs to the unfinished business they left when Nikki came to the door. They still had to look for the missing keys and figure out what to do with the Royal. It had an evilness about it that was really starting to scare them. They also wondered how Nikki could have known about it. Carol must have overheard Isobel talking with someone about it and told Nikki. That was the only explanation they could come up with, unless Nikki was spying on them the entire time. Maybe she was already at Isobel's house and heard the conversations between Isobel and Carissa.

Yes, that has to be it! They definitely have to get rid of it now!

After searching Isobel's bedroom for the missing keys with no luck, the women sat side by side on the bed.

"I don't think I want this thing here anymore," Isobel said.

"What do you mean?" Carissa asked. "What do you want to do with it?"

Isobel looked at the machine with furious eyes, "I think I want to get rid of it. It has caused nothing but trouble since I have had it, and the previous...," she stopped herself.

Carissa looked at her in confusions, "Previous what?"

"Nothing," she answered, "it doesn't matter anymore. Will you help me get this thing out of here?"

Carissa had reservations about the idea but agreed to help anyway. Without any further conversation, the two of them hoisted it up and carried it to the top of the stairs (which they knew were going to be a nightmare to carry the machine down). They put it down, both out of breath. With Carissa in front, stepping backwards down the steps, and Isobel behind, they very cautiously traveled down the three-story staircase awkwardly with the weighty machine. They almost dropped it a couple of times while its weight kept shifting with each step.

Isobel decided she wanted to get rid of it in a nearby lake. She said they should just be able to drop it in the water. The weight of it would surely sink it straight to the bottom with no chance of resurfacing.

The plan was simple.

The plan was to walk out deep enough into the water to hide the Royal.

The plan was to make a quick escape when the task was finished.

The plan was to not turn back.

The plan was NOT to have someone watching them from behind a tree.

When Nikki emerged from behind the tree, she took a hard look in all directions to make sure no one was watching her. When she was sure no one was around, she walked over to the exact spot where Isobel and Carissa had just dumped the typewriter she was so curious about. The place where the two women dropped the machine was easy to spot because there were still a lot of tiny bubbles circling on the water's surface that had not had time to settle.

Nikki took her shoes off and went into the water. She found the Royal at the bottom of the lake when she kicked it with her bare toes, sending a jolt of pain through her foot and up into her calf. "Damn it," she said as she picked up her foot and rubbed her toes.

She knew she would have to go under the water in order to accomplish her task, so she let her foot go, pinched her nose with the fingers on her right hand, and dropped herself down below the water's surface. She knew immediately that holding her nose was mute because she needed both hands to lift the Royal out of the water. Nikki was fourteen years old and pretty strong so she was able to do it on her own, but she struggled. Getting it *home* would be the problem.

When she got to the edge of the lake, she put the typewriter down and sat next to it (without knowing another girl would sit in that same spot with that same machine three years later), and tried to figure out how she was going to get it home. She looked at Buddy as if he knew what she should do, but he just started to lick the water off her hands.

Nikki knew her dad was home napping. He was always tired from working so much, which was part of the reason her parents split up. She knew she could take his car and get it home, but that would require her to leave the typewriter on the embankment until she got back. She only debated for a minute before starting a full sprint, with her dog, to her house to get the car. It was her only option.

It was a piece of cake. Nikki's dad was asleep and his car keys were on the coffee table in the living room. She grabbed them, ran back out the door, and drove back to the lake. Her dad taught her how to drive about a year prior (even though she was not old enough to get her license), and she was pretty good at it.

She drove the car right out into the grass and up to where the typewriter was. It was still there, waiting for her. Nikki parked the car, loaded it up, and took it home where she got it into her bedroom rather easily. The Patterson's lived in a one-story home, so she didn't have any steps to contend with.

Nikki put it right on her dresser and covered it up with a white sheet. Her parents hardly ever went into her room so she figured they wouldn't see it. After she had it all set up, she called her mom.

The phone rang four times before Carol answered. "Hi Nikki," she sounded a little better, "is everything okay?"

"Yeah Mom. Do you know when you'll be home?"

"I am still waiting to talk with the doctor," she said, "He should be in any time now. Just hang tight hun It won't be long, I promise."

After Carol made a promise to her daughter that she wasn't sure she would be able to keep, she ended the call. She did not want Nikki to hear her cry, and she could feel the tears welling up in her eyes. She knew she would not be released until she told the doctor she did not have any hallucinations and that she was fine. She knew the only reason she was there was because they thought she was crazy. She didn't appear to have any injuries related to her accident, so there would be no reason not to let her go home, as long as she kept her cool and did not start talking about the bees again.

But the bees were there! The blood was there! The opening in my arm, where the insects flew out, it was there!

5 7

After a long day and feeling relieved because the Royal was gone, Isobel sat down to relax and watch the news. Carissa had gone home and Isobel was left alone to open a brand-new bottle of Kendall Jackson pinot noir, her usual stress reliever at the end of a hard day. With her freshly poured glass of wine, she looked at the TV and the headline news story got her attention right away.

There was a pedestrian struck by a car near the area she used to work. It wasn't surprising because all the news shows ever reported anymore were tragic events and depressing stories. The reporter on TV was talking about the accident while the camera person zoomed in on a section of the shoulder of highway eighty-four where there was a little black car. Isobel could not tell what kind of car it was, but it looked familiar.

As the news story unfolded, Isobel finished her first glass of wine and poured a second one. The woman reporting stated the names of the people who were involved in the accident, and Isobel gasped as her heart skipped a beat when she heard the name, Carol Patterson.

Isobel turned the volume up on the TV just in time to hear that Carol was the one who hit someone. The poor woman was run over and killed instantly, and when they disclosed the name of that person, Isobel took in another deep breath as she realized her typewriter was responsible for another death.

Elisabeth Burkhart was her name. Even though the news was so new, the broadcast had interviewed some of the dead woman's friends, one of them being a woman who only knew her a little because they were neighbors. That woman, who they didn't even name, stated that every time she saw Liz she was walking her dog on their street, but she always had her face glued to her cell phone. Texting and walking was as popular as texting and driving with most people, unfortunately. That little bit of information was important because there were witnesses who stated the woman walking on the shoulder of the road was looking at her cell phone and not paying attention to anything around her.

Isobel started to think the worst. Carol's accident *had* to be related to the Royal. She knew Carissa had the typewriter just after she found out Carol was screwing around with her husband. Maybe she wasn't finished with the typewriter yet, or maybe *it* was not finished with *her*. She did not know what to do or what to think, but one thing was for sure; she had to get the Royal back as soon as possible.

The news story ended while Isobel was tripping over her thoughts, so she missed the tail end of it. She looked at the half-finished glass of red wine in her hand and went into the kitchen to dump it out. She had to be clear-minded while she thought about her next move.

She knew whatever it was going to be, she would have to do it alone. She could not risk getting anyone else involved in her dilemma anymore.

Isobel went to bed and actually got a good night's sleep that night. Not only did she have a slight buzz from the wine, but her room was at a comfortable temperature. She slept soundly, until she was awakened by the annoying sound of her alarm clock (*beep, beep, beep*) at seven the next morning. She got out of bed and was ready to tackle her task for the new day, bringing that machine back into her house. The typewriter was not something she wanted anymore due to all of the trouble it was causing, but if she did not go get it, someone else might. Then, the trouble would only get worse. Isobel shuddered at the thought.

The Typewriter made her nervous, but Nikki approached it slowly after closing and locking her bedroom door behind her. She could not risk anyone knowing she had it, especially her mom, and she had no idea when she might get home from the hospital. Nikki stood in front of the Royal and just stared at the sheet she had thrown over top of it, afraid to remove it, but she knew what she had to do. The reason she took the thing in the first place was to even the score. She was tired of seeing her mom cry.

Nikki was a pretty private person, mostly because she had nothing in common with her peers, or her neighbors. With no one to talk to, except her mom, nobody knew she stole the typewriter. No one knew about her mom's daily crying ever since she found out Bill was seeing someone else, and no one knew she overheard her mom on the phone talking about someone named Carissa. No one knew that Nikki *knew* Carissa was the woman Bill was seeing. They didn't know Nikki overheard Isobel talking to her mom about what her typewriter had done, and no one knew how much Nikki loved her mom, and would do anything for her, but they were about to find out.

She lifted the sheet off the machine and sat in a chair in front of it. Not knowing where to start or what to do, she simply started typing. As her fingers found the keys she started to notice something strange. It was like her fingers knew where to go before she directed them, and after a little while, she was not even in charge of her hands. The keys sort-of moved through her, but on their own. She knew what she wanted to accomplish before she sat down to type, but she didn't know exactly how she was going to do it. That didn't matter because the typewriter knew exactly what to do as Nikki just looked on.

After a few pages were typed, Nikki's fingers just stopped. Not knowing what to do at that point, she got up from her seat and went out of her bedroom to get a soda, which was when she got the call from Carol. Apparently, she was being released from the hospital and would be home in about an hour. Nikki went back into her room when she hung up the phone and covered up the Royal and the typed pages, without having a chance to see what she had typed.

Nikki's dog, Buddy, was scratching at her bedroom door, a normal act when he wanted to go outside. She grabbed a coat because it was pretty cold outside and took Buddy for a much-needed walk. They went around the entire block, which was something Nikki needed as well to try to clear her head and figure out what had just happened. She could not, for the life of her, remember what she typed on that machine. She knew her goal was to get even with Carissa, but what did she type? What did *it* type?

Carol stayed home from work for the rest of that week, mostly because she was upset, not because she was hurt. She still had no idea what happened. She knew what she saw, but there was no evidence of anything like that happening to her arm. She knew the police probably thought she made it up to explain how she could have hit that woman on the road. Carol was actually pissed when she found out the woman was texting and walking in the road. That was something Carol could not stand, how the world was so connected electronically and no one actually talked to each other anymore.

She enjoyed her time home with her daughter that week, and she actually got a lot done around the house. Nikki's dad had gone home to an apartment he was temporarily staying in. He stayed at the house with Nikki until he knew Carol was coming home. They were divorced, but continued to have a good relationship for Nikki's sake.

One interesting thing that happened the week when Carol was home was that she received an invitation to the company Christmas party. She knew Carissa had to be the one to send it because Carol was in charge of the party arrangements, and would not have sent herself an invitation. Actually, after everything that happened, she didn't even want to go to the party. She was pretty sure she was going to decline. She did not want to be in the same room with Carissa while they were partying and drinking. Carol wasn't very good at hiding her feelings and she knew that she might get into it with Carissa over Bill, even though she never intended to go out with him again.

When the weekend arrived, Carol decided she wanted to take Nikki out to breakfast because she felt like she had neglected her daughter lately. Nikki always slept in on Saturday mornings so Carol tapped lightly on her closed bedroom door. When she got no answer, and heard no movement from the other side of the door, she decided to do something she did not normally do. She just walked in.

At first, she didn't see it because she walked straight over to Nikki's bed and tapped her on the shoulder to wake her up. Nikki kept the curtains closed, so it was dark in her room, even though the sun was shining brightly outside. Nikki jumped at her mother's touch as if she was awakened from a bad dream. She immediately got out of bed and stood with her back facing the typewriter, trying to hide it.

"What?" She asked her mom.

"I'm sorry for waking you," Carole said, "But I thought I would take you to breakfast."

Nikki took her mom's arm and slowly directed her back toward the door so she wouldn't look at the table with the Royal on in. "Sure. Just give me a few minutes to get ready."

Carol agreed and surprisingly made it out of Nikki's bedroom without seeing the Royal. Nikki breathed a sigh of relief as she knew she had just dodged a bullet. How would she have explained that one?

The ladies went to breakfast at Denny's and had a nice chat about how things were going in both of their lives, all the while Nikki was thinking about how to get rid of the typewriter without being noticed. She got lucky when Carol mentioned that she wanted to go to the grocery store after breakfast. That would be her chance, and she convinced her mom to take her home first.

Isobel tried to call Carissa three times and got her voicemail each time. She could not leave a message. This was too important and the two of them really needed to talk. The fourth time was a charm as Carissa finally answered the phone.

"What's up Isobel?" She knew who it was by the name displayed on her caller I.D.

"Have you seen the news?" Isobel immediately went into the reason she was calling. "I can't believe it!"

"No," Carissa said, but she had a feeling she knew what her friend was talking about because she had seen it first-hand, "What's up?"

"Carol hit someone with her car. I don't know if *she* was hurt, but the woman she hit died!" Carissa was crying.

She paused for a few seconds before responding, "No! She did not come back to work so I don't know how she is?"

It had been a couple of days since the accident and Carissa never really watched the news. She had no idea someone was killed that day. A chill ran through her body as she listened to Isobel.

"Don't you see?" Isobel said, "It's our fault. I know you typed and wished harm to Carol through my typewriter, but we got an innocent person killed!" She was yelling now. "What the hell are we going to do?"

"Do you know who is was?" Carissa asked, not sure if she wanted to hear the answer.

"Some woman named Liz, or Elizabeth," Isobel's voice had settled down as she suddenly remembered the letters. "On my God!" she almost dropped her phone. "Do you remember the missing letters?"

"What are you talking about?"

"That day at my house when the three keys were missing from the keyboard of the typewriter." Isobel sounded desperate, "they spelled Liz!"

"Oh, c'mon Isobel," Carissa tried to persuade her, even though she knew it was true, "That doesn't mean anything."

"Are you kidding me?" Isobel was getting mad, "of course it does. This it too big of a coincidence to actually *be* a coincidence."

"I have to go Isobel," Carissa said, "Bill is on his way home and I have to talk to him."

They ended their phone call and Isobel hoped Carissa was not planning on confronting Bill about his affair. At least, she hoped she wouldn't tell him *how* she found out. Isobel did not want to be involved any further.

Isobel stepped outside. She wanted to check her mail to get her mind off things, but as soon as the chilly air hit her, she went back inside to grab a jacket. Dressed appropriately, she ventured back out and made it to her mailbox, where there was an envelope dressed in holiday cheer waiting for her. Curious, she opened it. It was an invitation to the annual Humphrey's Homes Christmas party. She wondered why she got an invitation when she didn't work there anymore. She smiled and walked back into her house. At least for a few minutes, she had something else to think about, other than the fact that she absolutely had to get the Royal back somehow, and she had to do it before anyone else got hurt.

A few days went by without incident as Isobel let the dust settle a little to allow herself time to digest everything. She knew she had to go get the Royal out of the lake, but she was not sure how she was going to pull that off all by herself. Not only was it getting colder outside every day as winter approached, but she was also nowhere near strong enough to lift that piece of heavy machinery and carry it home. She had a car she was going to put it in, but she had to get it from the water to the car, and from the car to her house once she got it in the driveway. All of this, she planned on doing without being noticed. She knew the feat was going to be difficult, but the more she thought about it, the more she decided she could do it, and the more she knew she *had* to do it. With her car keys in-hand, she went out the front door, got in her car, and drove to the lake.

The water was still and the air was silent as Isobel approached the edge of the water. She knew exactly where she and her friend had dropped the demon. She looked ahead of her as she kicked off her shoes (she forgot to put her sneakers on and was not about to ruin her good moccasins) and stepped into the ice-cold water.

She slowly waded out until she was about three feet away from the spot she knew she would find the typewriter, when she felt something brush against her calf

251

so gently that she wasn't sure if it was actually something like a fish, or just the water swirling underneath the surface as she moved through it. She shrugged it off and took another step, where she felt the sensation again, but this time, it was on the opposite side and it was against her thigh. It made her flinch.

Isobel was scared and turned to go back. She intended to go back out, but as soon as she lifted her right foot to take a step, something (or someone) grabbed it and pulled on her leg with such force it pulled her under the surface of the water. Before she knew it, her mouth and nose were completely engulfed with rushing water that was whirl pooling around her entire body. She tried to scream, but the sound was muffled by thousands of bubbles that rushed out of her nose and mouth, and only caused more water to enter her throat.

She was of sound enough mind to know she was in serious trouble as she desperately tried to reach the water's surface in order to let her voice be heard. The water was fairly shallow, so it was surprising she was pulled so far under, but with her eyes open she could see the light above the water and reached for it as she was being pulled farther and farther into the lake.

Isobel knew she had finally reached the surface when she felt the chill of the brisk air on her right hand as she continued to swing her left hand at what appeared to be nothing under the water. She had no idea what she was battling, but it had become a life or death situation for her. She continued to thrash around in the water as her free hand made waves and her head was bobbing up and down, giving her the chance to gain quick breaths of air.

She continued to scream as she fought for her life. She kicked and found nothing but the rocks on the lake's floor with either of her feet. Her legs and feet were beat up by rocks and what was probably glass, which cut through her feet and ankles. She waved her arms around aimlessly and they hit nothing.

Battered and bruised, Isobel found enough strength and directed it all to her legs as she planted both of her feet on the ground and pushed up as hard as she could, breaking through the invisible beast, and thrust her body upward toward the sunlight that was shining in beams down through the water. In that moment, she gained enough strength to get her head out of the water, just for a second, as she screamed as loud as she could, gaining the attention of a passerby.

Kenneth Wright was on his way home. He had walked to the local Wawa for his mother. She needed some soda and he always volunteered to help his parents. He was a good-mannered teenager, but he also just wanted to get out of the house this particular day. He didn't have a lot of friends, being the local sheriff's kid, but that was okay with him. He liked his solitude and he went on frequent walks by himself to gain the peacefulness he enjoyed.

Kenneth was walking, swinging his shopping bag with his arm, when the sound of the still air and quietness was interrupted by, what he thought was a woman screaming. He quickly turned his head in the direction the sound came from and all he could see was splashing water in the lake. It was like there was a large fish playing on the surface, which he knew couldn't be the case. The largest fish they had in the lake in Hollow Creek were sunnies, and maybe a few catfish.

Curious, he ran toward the water. He saw nothing as he approached, but then, suddenly it appeared again. Only, this time he knew it was not a fish. It was a person. He started to run toward the lake as fast as he could and when he got to the edge of the water, he ran right into it. The force of the water immediately slowed him down, but he fought his way through it until he reached her.

She was exhausted from fighting and her body started to go limp by the time Kenneth reached her. He grabbed the only part of her that he could see because it was on the surface; it was her arm. He pulled her up above the water and could not tell if she was conscious as her eyes were closed and she lay lifeless in his arms.

Kenneth, only being fourteen years of age, was scared to death as he dragged her out of the water and to the grass. He reached for his cellphone, which was in his pocket, but discovered it was dead due to being water logged. He knew he had to get help, and he knew who was lying in front of him now that she was out of the water. It was his neighbor, Mrs. Parrish.

Not knowing what to do, Kenneth ran to the nearest house and found Mr. Harrison, a neighbor he barely knew, outside starting up his lawn mower. He thought, for a brief moment, that if Mr. Harrison had been outside five minutes earlier, he would have been the one to hear her screams and Kenneth would not be in this situation.

Kenneth yelled to get Mr. Harrison's attention and it took a couple of times, but his hollers were finally heard. The man turned off his mower and asked Kenneth what was wrong. As Kenneth tried to explain, but he was too out of breath to get his words out, Mr. Harrison noticed the woman lying on the ground by the lake and the two of them ran down to Isobel's side.

Mr. Harrison threw his cellphone to Kenneth and told him to dial 911, and he started chest compressions on Isobel. He happened to be certified in CPR, but did not want to put Kenneth in that position, so he alternated giving breaths and chest compressions on her all by himself as Kenneth called for an ambulance.

Almost immediately, they heard the sirens. The fire station was just down the block so the paramedics arrived in just a few minutes. They relieved Mr. Harrison of his duties of saving the woman as they took over. Isobel started to cough almost as soon as they started working on her. They took her vitals and loaded her onto a gurney and rushed her into the back of their ambulance. They thanked Mr. Harrison and Kenneth before they drove off to the hospital.

Mr. Harrison offered to take Kenneth home, but he refused. He said he would rather walk to clear his head. Kenneth's body was still shaking for the entire walk home from a combination of his wet clothes in the cold air, and the fact that he had just gone through the scariest thing he had ever experienced.

A few days later, Isobel woke up in a hospital room with no recollection of how she had gotten there. She had tubes hooked into her arm which were pumping fluids into her. Confused, she looked around the room. She saw no one and heard nothing but the steady beeping of some machine that was next to her, which she assumed was a heart monitor. She looked at her arm and noticed blood soaking through some gauze that was wrapped around a needle that was inserted into her arm. She started to get restless as she did not know how she got there.

She noticed some Christmas decorations around the room which brought back a memory of her receiving the invitation to a Christmas party in the mail. Then the memories started flooding into her brain like the water that flooded her throat when she nearly drowned. She remembered the water. She remembered the struggle. She even remembered the reason she was at the lake in the first place, to get the typewriter.

She grabbed the call button that was lying on a table next to her, and buzzed for the nurse, who came in immediately. The nurse called for a doctor right away since that was the first time Isobel had woken up and she would need to be evaluated.

"What happened," Isobel asked. "How did I get here."

The nurse, who looked extremely timid and confused, was just about to say something when the doctor walked in. She proceeded to check Isobel's vital signs, while the doctor briefly looked over some papers that were attached to a clipboard.

"How are you feeling, Ms,,," he looked back down at the clipboard, "Parrish."

Isobel looked at him, narrowing her eyebrows at the fact that he did not even know her name.

"I'm okay. How did I get here, and when can I go home?"

"You have been through a traumatic experience and almost drowned." He shuffled through his papers again, "We will have to keep you here for a couple of days for observation."

"No!" she snapped at him, "I can't stay here!"

Before the doctor could speak again, a nurse from the nurse's station came into the room and told Isobel she had a couple of visitors. She could not, for the life of her, think of who it could be. The only person she thought it might be was Carissa.

Isobel looked at the nurse questioningly. "Please send them in."

She could not believe it when Carol and her daughter Nikki slowly entered the room. Nikki did not look at her; she just stared at the floor while Carol walked right up to the side of her bed. "We heard about what happened."

Isobel, not even knowing what day it was, asked,

"Well then can you tell me please? I only remember bits and pieces and no one around here is telling me anything," she gave an angry look to the doctor.

"What were you doing in the lake?" Carol asked, "Word travels fast in our town."

Nikki backed away from Isobel's bedside and headed toward the door. She almost got there when her mom stopped her. "Where are you going honey?"

Nikki looked like a frightened puppy when she looked up at her mom and Isobel. "I'm sorry," she said and started to cry. "I didn't mean to cause any trouble."

"Nikki, what are you talking about," Carol asked.

"I just wanted to help," she said, "I know why you were at the lake Mrs. Parrish." Nikki looked back down at the floor, "It's not there anymore."

Isobel suddenly remembered what happened. She went to the lake to get the Royal, but the details of what happened that day were fuzzy. "What do you mean, it's not there?"

"I took it," she said. She was shaking. "I wanted to help my mom. I heard what that thing could do."

Carol looked at the two of them in confusion. "What are you..."

Her words were interrupted by Isobel's panic. "What did you do Nikki?"

All Nikki could say was, "I'm sorry..." She searched for something else to say, but could not find the words.

"Oh my God!" Isobel yelled, "I have to get out of here. What is the date today?" She knew the date for the Christmas party for Humphrey's Homes had to be getting close.

"December 21st," the doctor interrupted.

That's all Isobel had to hear. She started tugging at her I.V. and asked the doctor where her clothes were.

"What are you doing," he asked, "you need to stay here until we know you are okay to be discharged." He grabbed her wrist where the I.V. site was in an attempt to stop her.

"YOU CAN'T FUCKING KEEP ME HERE!" she screamed at him. "WHERE ARE MY CLOTHES?"

"Calm down Ms. Parrish," he said.

"FUCK YOU!" she screamed as she ripped her I.V. out of her arm leaving a trail of blood on the white sheets that she struggled to get out of. "Carol, can you take me home?"

Carol agreed, but Nikki interrupted her, "Mom," she said, "we should probably take her to our house."

"Why?" Isobel asked.

Nikki looked down at the floor again, "Because the typewriter is in my room."

The doctor ordered the nurse to go get discharge papers for Isobel, but Isobel was dressed and out the door with Carol and Nikki before the papers could be drawn up.

When they got outside, it was cold and dark. Isobel asked Carol, "Aren't you going to the Christmas party?"

"No," Carol said, "I'm not up to it this year."

The three of them got in Carol's car and drove to the Patterson's house.

The women pulled into the driveway and the house was completely dark. There were no lights on because it had been light outside when Carol and Nikki drove to the hospital. December had a way of going from light to dark in a matter of minutes early in the evening.

Carol got out of the car and opened the back door for Nikki. She still insisted on having the child locks on, even though Nikki was a teenager. They walked to the front door and Carol immediately turned on the front light and the living room light so they could see, although Isobel wasn't worried about that. She just wanted to get her typewriter.

"Where is it," she asked Nikki.

"This way," she directed the women down the hallway.

They all walked into Nikki's dark room where they could not see a thing. Nikki reached for the light switch and the second she flipped it on, she gasped.

"I swear, it was there!" Nikki pointed to her desk where the Royal had been. Now, the only thing there was the white sheet.

Nikki and Carol both looked back at Isobel, who fled from the room. They said nothing as Isobel ran out their front door.

Isobel ran all the way home without looking back.

She had to change into nice clothes so she could make an appearance at the party she did not want to go to, but she had to warn Carissa. She knew what Nikki meant when she said she wanted to help her mom.

She opened the front door, dropping her keys twice because she was so freaked out, and ran up the steps to her bedroom, where the door was closed. She did not remember closing it. But, she wasn't remembering a lot these days.

She fumbled with the door handle and, again, was faced with a pitch-black room. She didn't have the luxury of having a light switch right by the door, so she had to walk into the dark room and find her table lamp, the one that sat on the table where she kept the Royal.

Isobel found the lamp, turned it on, and screamed at the horror that was right in front of her.

The Royal was on the table in front of her. It was exposed with a blank sheet of paper loaded into it. Although she was disquieted by the sight of it, knowing she had dumped it in the lake, Isobel had a party to get ready for. She quickly grabbed a nice dress out of her closet and jumped in the shower to wash away the hospital gunk.

She was only in the shower for five minutes when the water turned ice cold and she jumped back in the tub to get out of its streaming path. She reached through the water (trying not to let it touch her body too much) for the lever to turn the water off. She got ahold of it, turned the water off, and yanked the towel off the towel rack that was right next to the shower. Isobel was shivering as she wrapped herself in the towel and blotted herself dry.

It didn't take long for her to notice how cold it was in the bathroom. Drying herself off was not warming her up. With the towel wrapped around her and firmly tucked in just above her breast to keep it from falling down, she left the bathroom and went into her bedroom, where she thought it would be warmer for her, so she could get dressed. As soon as she stepped into her room, her plan changed. She could not believe what she saw.

The Royal's paper was no longer blank. Isobel just stared at it while she inched closer to it to see what it said. She was trembling on top of her shivers as she approached the demon. Her heart jumped into her throat when she saw it. The paper before her simply read:

C A R I S S A.

She could only stare at the single sheet of white paper protruding from the top of her typewriter as her eyes burned and flooded with tears. Her hands quickly moved to cover her mouth as she gasped and shook, as her body was completely stricken with terror.

"NOOO!" She screamed at the machine. "That's not right! What did you do?" She sobbed and pleaded as if she was going to get an answer. Her entire face fell into her hands as she dropped to her knees. "Please take it back! Oh my God! PLEASE TAKE IT BACK!"

She screamed, but she knew her pleas were not going to change anything. There was nothing she could do.

After crying hysterically on the floor for a few minutes, she stood up and began to frantically pace back and forth across her bedroom. Things did not go the way she planned. She continued to cry as she searched for answers as to what she could do. How could she fix this? Was it too late? She kept asking herself these questions over and over again, but she already knew the answers. The problem could *not* be fixed because it *was* too late.

This isn't fair. I tried to get rid of you, didn't I? I put you in the fucking lake! Now, what the hell am I going to do? What the hell did you do?

Isobel became enraged because she knew she had to do something. This was all her fault and she knew it, so she went into her closet to look for something that would help her release her anger, and in her fit of rage, she pulled her clothes off the hangers and threw them all over the floor. She picked up several pairs of shoes, as well as the clothes that were strewn all over the closet floor, and threw them outside the closet door until her bedroom was so covered she could barely see the mahogany hardwood floor underneath.

A tiny bead of sweat dripped into her eye as she turned to pick up the last thing she could possibly throw, a pair of snow boots. She reached for them, and that's when she saw it, the answer to her problem, or at least she thought.

She had forgotten about the crowbar. She left it in the closet the day she pried the Royal typewriter out of its crate (it was packed in there so tightly when she moved to Hollow Creek). Her eyes widened as she slowly reached into the corner and picked up the curved piece of steel with both hands. It was cold to the touch, but she barely noticed the way it felt in her grasp as she turned to face the opening that led out of the closet and into her bedroom. She did not take her eyes off her shaking hands as she inched closer and closer to the doorway.

The room was so cold her hands began to shiver

uncontrollably, and for just one second, she almost lost her grip on what was soon to be her salvation. Refusing to let it drop, she quickly regained her composure and proceeded toward the closet doorway.

The typewriter was right where she left it, on the desk with that same single sheet of paper sticking out of it, the one that spelled out her friend's demise. As she stepped over the piles of clothing, she immediately felt a cold breeze pass by her. It was so cold in her room she could see her breath with each exhale. She made her way over the piles of dresses and shoes to the place where the Royal sat, almost looking at her. At that moment, she wished she had never found the damned thing that had ruined her life, and the lives of those around her.

As she glared at the piece of machinery that had made her life a living hell over the last few months, she knew she had the only solution in her hand. She reached back over her head with her right arm while holding the crowbar so tight that, even though she was so cold, perspiration had formed in her hand making it difficult to maintain her grip. She grabbed the end of it with her other hand to get a better hold on it before pulling it down with everything she had inside of her and smashing it straight into the center of the keyboard of the beast before her.

Realizing the impact barely made a dent in the typewriter with only the "H" and "J" keys falling through the center making a small hole in the keyboard, she swung her arms back to land a second blow, which came down right next to the hole she had already created. This time, the crowbar went right through the keys and hit the surface below.

She continued to smash the crowbar into the machine over and over again as keys, pieces of the roller, and debris from the base of it flew everywhere. Isobel could not control herself as she continued to destroy every mechanism within the Royal until, suddenly, her arm stopped in midair.

She stood frozen for a moment, and with one sudden burst, her bedroom window smashed inward and hundreds of tiny pieces of glass flew into her room and scattered on the floor around her.

She looked at the window and then back at the broken typewriter and she noticed there was still one thing intact as it lay flat on the table, the paper with the letters on it. She tried to reach for it, but she could not move her arms. Something held her back as she attempted to collect that fateful piece of paper so she could rip it to shreds.

She was still trying to move when a cold wind funneled in through the window and the bits of typewriter started to move. Isobel thought the wind was causing them to flutter a little on the desktop, but she became terrified as she watched the Royal's broken pieces start to elevate themselves above the table.

Before she had time to react, the cool breeze picked up the fragments of the typewriter, along with the shards of glass from the broken window, and before she knew it, she was in a tornado of debris that lifted her off the floor and moved her slowly toward the window. She tried to scream but nothing came out. She could not move. She could not yell. She was trapped!

It moved her closer and closer to the window before a sudden blast of air and glass picked her up and threw her out of the third-floor window, dropping her to the earth.

A sudden stillness took over Isobel's bedroom.

Sergeant Snyder was home the night the screams were heard from his neighbor's house. He and his family had just finished dinner when he heard the sound of broken glass. He jerked his head in the direction of Isobel's house, and quickly went to his back door to look outside. Kenneth stood nearby and watched as his father stepped out into the darkness.

Sergeant Snyder called for back-up when he saw the broken glass on the ground behind his neighbor's house. Kenneth followed him outside, but was quickly told to go back inside and stay with his mother.

He heard the sirens approaching as he walked over to the glass, where he looked up and noticed the broken window above. Sergeant Snyder ran to the back door, which was locked so he went to the front. That door was not only unlocked, but the door was open a few inches. He went in with his gun pulled and aimed out in front of him.

"Mrs. Parrish?" He yelled, but his calls went unanswered.

When the other officers arrived, one of them went into the house where he was and they slowly climbed the steps together, calling Isobel's name with no luck in gaining a response.

The house was eerily quiet as they reached the

opening to the last bedroom on the third floor. They went in, still holding their guns out in front of them. What they saw made Sergeant Snyder immediately call for an ambulance.

There was no one around and the window was broken completely out. There was glass all over the floor as they stepped through it and made their way to the window. They looked out the window and down to the ground. The only thing that seemed undisturbed and in one piece was an old typewriter that sat on a small table by the window.

There was nothing on the ground below, except a bunch of glass. They continued to search the house for Isobel, but found nothing, so they proceeded to check the grounds around the house. Still, nothing...

The newspapers called it a suicide, possibly an abduction. No one knew what to make of that, so rumors began to circulate around Hollow Creek about the disappearance of Mrs. Parrish. Out of all of the rumors, the most popular story was that she jumped out her window and died.

Kenneth never told his parents, or anyone else, about the time he pulled Mrs. Parrish out of the lake. He felt his discretion would have been important to her, but he didn't know why, and after what happened the night of her disappearance, he thought it would be in his best interest as well. In the end, there was never a day when Kenneth didn't wonder what happened to the woman who lived next door.

Follow Julie Kent
for news, previews of upcoming books, and more!

Follow Julie on Facebook.
facebook.com/Julie Kent, author

Follow Julie on Twitter.
@juliekent_27

Follow Julie on Instagram.
juliekent_author/